LATHARN'S DESTINY

HIGHLANDER FATE BOOK SIX

STELLA KNIGHT

PRONUNCIATION GUIDE

Latharn - LA-urn
Eibhlin - EHV-leen
Floraidh - FLOR-ie
Aoife - EE-fyə
Tulach - TUL-uk
Padraig - PAW-drig
Neacal - NIY-kl
Gormal - GAU-rum-ul
Baigh - BIE
Crisdean - KREESH-jun
Ros - ROEZ
Aimil - AY-mil

CHAPTER 1

Present Day
Tairseach, Scottish Highlands

A light breeze tugged at Evelyn's cloak as she approached the ancient village of Tairseach. She expelled a deep breath as she took in its ruins; overgrown grass, a decrepit castle in the distance, the crumbling remains of old thatch-roofed homes.

To any other person, Tairseach would just look like an old crumbling village, a casualty of the long march of time. But Evelyn knew better. Tairseach wasn't just an ordinary old village. It was a portal through time.

She could recall with stark clarity the first time she'd come here years ago with her mother, when she was still a teenager. Then, she'd still been reeling in disbelief—and anger—at the crazy tale her mother had told her. Yet as soon as they'd arrived at Tairseach, she sensed something different about the place . . . something she couldn't explain.

And when she'd taken her first trip back through time, her suspicions had been confirmed.

Evelyn drew closer to the ancient village, hiking up the skirts of her fourteenth-century gown as she moved. She'd hidden her gown beneath a large cloak, grateful that it was late winter and didn't look too suspicious. She stopped, adjusting the coif she'd placed over her long red hair before continuing on. The first time she'd worn a medieval gown and coif she'd felt ridiculous. But now the clothing felt as natural as a pair of jeans and a comfy T-shirt.

It should make sense that she felt so comfortable in clothing from the past . . . because she herself was born in the past. She'd been born in the fourteenth century with the Gaelic name Eibhlin Aingealag O'Brolchan. Her mother was a time traveler born in the twenty-first century, and her father a fourteenth-century Highland noble.

Her mother had dropped this major bombshell on her when she was sixteen. Even today, a decade later, she could recall every detail of that moment: the fire crackling in the fireplace, the mug of hot tea in her mother's shaking hands, the deep crimson sweater her mother wore, the pitter-patter of rain on the living-room windows, her mother's low but desperate voice and the strain on her fine, elegant features.

"Your father is long dead, Evie," her mother had whispered. "Because he was born in the past, when I met him. In the year 1360."

Evelyn had reacted with disbelief and rage, not speaking to her mother for weeks afterward. But her mother was telling the truth; she'd traveled to the past by accident after getting lost during a solo hiking trip to the Highlands and stumbling across Tairseach. She had met, married and fallen in love with her soulmate in the past, only to return to the present after his tragic death with their infant in her arms, modernizing Eibhlin's name to Evelyn Angelica O'Brolchan.

It was only after her mother took her to Tairseach and they traveled to the past together that Evelyn had fully accepted her story. Guilt constricted her chest at the memory of her initial anger, but her mother had forgiven her.

"I wouldn't have believed me, either," her mother insisted.

It was with her mother's blessing that she'd traveled to the past on her own—but only when she reached adulthood. She'd taken her second trip to the past while she was in college and stayed for nearly a month before returning to her relieved mother.

This was her third trip to the past. Her mother, her only true anchor to the present, had died in a car accident several years ago. It was her loss that spurred Evelyn to return to the past, to carry out something she'd ached to do once she'd learned the circumstances of her father's death.

Determination quickened her pace as she entered Tairseach. She'd left her rental car about a mile behind and walked the rest of the way here. The last time she'd come here, she'd taken a cab from the nearest town, but the probing questions as to why she'd want to be dropped off here had become increasingly difficult to answer. People who couldn't travel through time couldn't see Tairseach; it just looked as if she were requesting a drop-off in a remote glen in the middle of the Highlands. She'd even feared the last cab driver would refuse to leave her, warning her that it got dangerously cold out here at night, and she might not be able to find her way back. Evelyn had to practically beg him to leave her here.

She straightened as she scanned the village, soon spotting what she was looking for. A small vortex of wind at the base of a crumbling cottage, disturbing the grass that surrounded it. The wind, she'd noticed, appeared in a different spot each time she'd traveled. It seemed to be the source of the power—the magic—that hurtled travelers through time.

Swallowing hard, she moved toward the vortex of wind. She closed her eyes, conjuring up every detail she could recall about the ruins of MacUisdean Castle and what it must have looked like during its heyday: its gleaming stone walls, the courtyard bustling with activity, horse-drawn carts

4

making their way in and out of its massive front gates.

But most of all, she thought of her true purpose in returning to the past—avenging her late father. Her determination swelled, and she continued to step forward, until a familiar swirling blackness claimed her, and the world around her disappeared.

1391
Scottish Highlands

WHEN THE WORLD righted itself around Evelyn, she took a deep breath, clutching her roiling belly. She thought that she'd gotten used to the aftermath of time travel, which was akin to leaping off a high-speed rollercoaster at its apex. But she still felt just as nauseous and shaken as the first time she'd traveled back in time with her mother, who had held her hair back as she vomited.

Once her stomach calmed, Evelyn looked up, relief spiraling through her. *This was it.* She'd made several scouting trips to this area in her own time, determined to get to the right place.

In the present day, this area was just a sprawling glen full of overgrown grass, with the tattered ruins of MacUisdean Castle in the distance.

Now, a dirt road snaked through the glen, and

the castle that loomed in the distance was no ruin. It stood tall and formidable, made of gray stone and turreted towers, looking every inch a living, breathing medieval castle.

This was the place where her parents had met and married. Where they had come for many feasts and gatherings as part of Clan MacUisdean. During her previous trips to the past, she'd not allowed herself to come here, knowing it would pain her to see the place where her father had died.

Ignoring the stab of grief and anger that pierced her at the thought of her father's murder, Evelyn adjusted her gown and straightened, mentally reviewing her plan before continuing forward.

Her heart picked up its pace as she drew closer to the castle and the hubbub that lay past its gates—horse-driven carts entering and leaving the court-yard, servants hauling sacks of grain inside, stable boys leading horses to the stables.

During her previous trips to the past, she'd avoided interacting with people though she'd learned the way of speaking during this time with language tutors over the years, and her modern accent was now barely detectable. She hoped that it was enough to pass muster, as she intended to not only interact—but live—among the people of this time as a castle servant.

Evelyn approached the open castle gates, trailing a horse-drawn cart and a handful of servants carrying sacks of what she assumed were grain or flour. She spotted two guards by the gate and tensed, hoping that she looked the part of a young female servant in her simple, brown wool gown and white-linen coif. She'd even taken care to tear a few holes in the gown to make it look worn and authentic.

Fortunately, there was enough incoming traffic to the courtyard that she was able to trail the other servants past the gates without much notice. She looked around, spotting more sacks of grain that rested near one of the castle entrances. She needed to blend in as soon as possible if her plan was going to work.

Picking up her pace, she moved over to one of the sacks and hefted it up, carrying it toward one of the castle's entrances. Once she got inside, she'd have to improvise to find the kitchens or the cellars to drop it off.

"Where are ye going, lass?"

Evelyn froze, turning to face a lanky, red-haired man who approached her with a frown.

"I'm taken this grain tae the kitchens," she said, lowering her head.

"Well, ye're heading tae the cellars," the man said with a scowl. "The kitchens are through that entrance," he continued, turning to point to another entryway.

"My apologies," she said, keeping her gaze trained on the ground.

The man just grunted and moved past her to head inside. Relieved that she'd survived her first —albeit brief—encounter, she turned and made her way to the entrance the man had directed her to.

Two young female servants entered ahead of her, and she followed them, hoping they were making their way to the kitchens.

"Deoridh ran off with the steward's son; they're probably long gone tae the Low Countries by now," one of the servants, a petite, fair-haired woman, was saying to her companion in a low voice. "Can ye believe it?"

"I donnae ken what he sees in Deoridh; she's a cow," the other servant returned with a snort.

"A cow who spreads her legs," the fair-haired servant said, with a low chuckle. "The steward's son is not the first she's lain with in the castle."

The women tittered as Evelyn's heart raced. This was perfect. If she could take this Deoridh's place, it would be easier to obtain a post as a servant here.

She followed the two gossiping servants into the sprawling kitchens, filled with even more servants who bustled to and fro—tending to the oven fires, chopping vegetables, sorting and storing grain, scrubbing the wood counters and stone floors.

"Over here!" a stout, balding man shouted from the corner, gesturing for her to approach with the grain. He raised an eyebrow, taking the sack from her.

"Bringing in grain is usually Tulach's duty," he

said, eyeing her with curiosity. "Have I seen ye before?"

"Deoridh arranged for me tae take her place," Evelyn said, thinking quickly.

But the man was already ignoring her, turning his focus to the sack and its contents.

"Ye said ye're replacing Deoridh?"

Evelyn whirled. A woman who looked to be in her fifties with graying dark hair and severe dark eyes stood behind her, eyeing her with a scowl.

"Aye," Evelyn said. "She said I could take her—"

"I donnae care for the details," the woman said, with a dismissive wave of her hand. "I'm Floraidh, the head maid in the kitchens. Ye can take her bed in the servants' quarters. Pay is handed out every day after sundown—ye can see the steward about that, just tell him ye're taking Deoridh's place. Now get tae it, lass; the undercook needs help kneading the barley dough for the bread."

Floraidh moved along to bark orders to another kitchen maid. Relief bloomed within her; that had gone smoother than she could have hoped for.

She moved toward the undercook, a harried-looking woman who gestured toward a thick mound of dough on the counter. Evelyn got to work, barely having time to come to terms with the fact that she was in the kitchens of a medieval castle, as she was given an assortment of tasks—from helping a young maid scrub down the counters with lye soap, assisting

9

the undercooks with chopping vegetables and sorting grains into boiling pots, to manually turning a roasting chicken on a spit over the oven fire.

By the time her workday had ended, exhaustion had seeped into her bones. She trailed the other female servants to their quarters, which was a cellar lit dimly with candlelight and filled with straw mattresses.

As she settled on the bed that Floraidh directed her to, the enormity of the task that lay before her settled in, and she felt the stirrings of doubt. She took a deep breath, repeating to herself the words she'd told herself in the days—the weeks, the months—before she'd traveled to this time.

I'm going to kill the man who murdered my father.

This hadn't always been her plan. When she'd first learned of the circumstances of her birth father's death and the reality of time travel, she'd fantasized about changing the past, of going back in time to warn him and her mother.

"I wanted to do that, Evelyn. Desperately," her mother had told her, her hazel eyes filled with anguish. "But the stiuireadh told me that some things can't be changed: your father's death was one of them. It was something that—in their words —time meant to happen. They warned me that if I tried to change what happened to him, there could be negative consequences for you and all types of dangerous ripple effects. And the only person I love more than your father is you. I couldn't risk it. As much as it has broken my heart, I've accepted that what happened was always meant to happen."

Evelyn closed her eyes at the memory, tears stinging her eyes. She had still stubbornly gone to see a stiuireadh, one of the druid witches who helped guide travelers through time, only to be told the same thing.

She'd decided that even if she couldn't change her father's death, she could avenge him. Her life in the present had been devoted to returning to the time in which she'd been born. She'd studied medieval history in college, taken horseback and archery lessons, even fencing lessons and fight training in case she ever needed to wield a sword.

Friendships and relationships had taken a back-seat to her intentions; even her mother had urged her to live her life in the present. But a burning desire to return to this time had driven Evelyn, to make things right—by avenging her father and her grief-stricken mother.

Her hand drifted to the pocket she had sown into her underdress, relieved to find the pouch of dried hemlock she'd sealed there. She set aside her doubt and repeated her vow to herself.

I will avenge my parents. Laird Steaphan MacUisdean will pay for what he's done.

CHAPTER 2

*A*s Latharn's horse pulled up to the small, thatch-roofed cottage on the edge of MacUisdean lands, he found three people lined up outside waiting for him. His grip tightened on the reins and a sudden swell of anxiety arose in his gut.

As a former servant, it was odd to have people waiting for him. But this was what his life would be like once he claimed his title as laird of MacUisdean Castle—and chieftain of Clan MacUisdean.

He'd recently learned that the parents who'd raised him weren't his true parents; they had once been servants of his birth parents, the laird and chieftain Seoras MacUisdean and Lady Beitris MacUisdean. His paternal uncle Steaphan had killed and betrayed his father, and his mother died while under imprisonment years later. His adopted mother had told him all this on her deathbed, telling him that his two cousins Padraig and Neacal were in conflict over who would take over leader-ship of the clan—which was his birthright.

He dismounted as one of the men, tall and broad shouldered, approached to take his horse, giving him a respectful nod. Another man, with gray-streaked auburn hair and warm brown eyes, stepped forward to greet him.

"Laird and Chieftain Latharn MacUisdean," the man said, giving him a respectful bow. "I'm Gormal; I've been the one corresponding with ye."

"Gormal," Latharn said, giving the man a wide smile, though he felt disconcerted at Gormal already referring to him as laird and chieftain.

Gormal had once served as a close advisor to his father. He'd fled MacUisdean lands after his murder and had taken up work as a steward in the manor of a noble on the adjoining lands of Clan Creagach. He'd known Latharn's adoptive parents, and was one of the few people who'd known that he was alive. His uncle had killed his older brothers, and it was assumed that Latharn, who'd been just a babe, had died, but his birth mother had managed to smuggle him out of the castle.

Latharn had contacted Gormal by letter after learning of his true identity; Gormal had arranged to secretly house Latharn on the outskirts of MacUisdean lands as he prepared to gather men over to his side.

"Many of us have never given up hope that ye'd return tae claim yer birthright," Gormal was saying now. "Welcome home, my laird."

Latharn had to stop himself from correcting Gormal, reminding himself that the title was his birthright—the title he'd come to claim.

"I thank ye," Latharn said gruffly.

"This is Horas, he'll serve as yer guard until ye have more men on yer side," Gormal said, gesturing to the man who had taken his horse.

Latharn stilled in surprise as Horas stepped forward, withdrawing his sword and kneeling before him, giving him a solemn look.

"As yer father had my sword, ye'll have mine," Horas pledged.

Latharn just gave him a nod, uncertain of how to respond to such fealty.

"And this young lassie is Aoife, she'll serve as yer personal maid until ye're back in the castle where ye belong," Gormal said, gesturing to a mousy, straw-haired lass who hovered by the entrance of the cottage.

Latharn almost wanted to tell Gormal that he didn't need a personal maid but held his tongue. He would soon have a host of servants; it was something else he'd have to get used to.

"'Tis not much," Gormal said apologetically, as he escorted Latharn inside the cottage. "I had to give up my finer home once yer father was overthrown; my family and I once lived here. My wife and I now live in our grown son's former home; he moved down tae Edinburgh. My wee bairns have all grown, but I've kept this cottage for their use when they come tae the Highlands."

Latharn took it in. It consisted of a large main room with a hearth and an area for dining, two other doors that led to small bedrooms, and a shuttered window.

"'Tis more than enough," Latharn said, waving away his apology. It relieved him that he was staying in a simple home; it was what he was used to. He had grown up in a cottage that didn't look too different from this one.

"'Tis not what ye deserve as our true laird," Gormal returned, with a fierce scowl. "I will do whatever I can tae help ye; ye have my word. A man I trust has taken over my post while I work with ye tae reclaim yer titles. Yer parents—the ones by birth, and the ones who adopted ye—were good people. 'Tis an honor tae help their son claim his birthright."

Gormal gave him another reverential look; Latharn made himself hold his gaze. Would he ever get used to such unbridled loyalty—the same loyalty he'd shown the man he'd served, Artair Dalaigh, during his years as a servant? He knew from what his mother had told him that his birth father was a good man: a strong warrior, admired and revered. How could he hope to follow such a man? A man he'd never known?

Ye will, he told himself. *Ye must.* He needed to push aside his stirrings of doubt and act the part of a leader, even if he didn't yet feel like one. It was what he needed to do if he expected men to follow him.

"I thank ye," he repeated, wishing he had something more profound to say. "Once I get settled, I'll need tae speak tae—"

"I've already handled it," Gormal interrupted. "As soon as I got yer letter, I started tae plan. There was contention over which of Steaphan's sons would become laird; many in the clan whisper of Padraig's cruelty. I feared there would be a battle over it. But the lairdship went tae Padraig, the oldest son, despite his lack of honor. I've kept yer arrival hidden; Padraig doesnae ken ye're here, and I'll make certain it remains that way until ye're ready tae fight him for yer titles. A clan noble by the name of Baigh—who's still loyal tae yer father— will visit ye here on the morrow. I've also arranged for a couple of servants I ken at the castle tae spy on yer behalf. Ah, we have much tae do, my laird. But for now, I urge ye tae rest. Aoife has already prepared yer bed and will make ye a meal," Gormal said. "And Laird MacUisdean," he continued, his voice wavering with emotion, "'tis good tae have ye home."

Latharn felt overwhelmed by this onslaught of information, but merely gave him a polite nod. Gormal left him alone after giving him another bow, and Aoife began to silently move about the small cooking area to prepare him a meal.

Resisting the urge to help her, Latharn moved over to the window, opening the shutters to look out at the lands that was his by birthright: vast glens

17

lightly bit by frost, a line of forests on the horizon, snowcapped mountains in the distance.

If he succeeded, he would rule over these lands and the people who dwelled here. MacUisdean Castle would be his. Again, doubt constricted his chest. There was much he needed to learn about the intricacies of leadership. He had watched his laird Artair Dalaigh run his manor and the people who worked for him. He'd learned to fight under Artair's tutelage and then with the MacGreghor clan. But it wasn't enough to know how to fight, to have observed a fine leader. How could he learn to be a laird and chieftain when he'd only known life as a servant who followed others?

He thought of the family he'd always known: his adopted parents, who'd loved him as fiercely as if he were their own blood, and his four younger siblings—Crisdean, Iain, Anabal, Sineag. He was the closest to his younger brother Crisdean; he'd only told Crisdean his true name and what he intended to do. He'd made him swear not to tell their siblings yet. Latharn knew that all of them, even his two sisters, would want to fight on his behalf. But they had their own lives now, and he wouldn't allow any of them to come to harm on his behalf.

Latharn looked down, gripping the silver-gilded brooch he'd pinned to his tunic.

"It belonged tae yer birth father," his adopted mother had told him, when she'd given it to him. "A gift from his father, and his father before him. Yer birth mother wanted me tae give it tae ye when the time was right."

He fingered the delicate filigree design of the brooch, wishing he could recall anything about his birth parents or the brothers who'd died. His mother had given him as much details as she could: his parents liked to laugh together, they were deeply in love despite their marriage being an arranged one. His father had been formidable yet well liked; his mother made certain that the castle servants were well cared for, especially during the harsh winters of the Highlands. His brothers, who were still lads when Steaphan had them murdered, had been fine hunters and jovial lads who enjoyed making their parents smile with their jests.

But hearing about those details didn't compare to having known them himself. Rage pulsed within him; if only he'd always known whom he truly was. If only he could have properly avenged his parents and killed Steaphan MacUisdean before he'd died of natural causes and old age—instead of spending his years in servitude.

Ye can avenge them by claiming the titles they bestowed upon ye, he told himself. *Ye can still make them proud.*

He returned his gaze to the lands that stretched beyond the cottage. The task that lay before him was daunting, but he would succeed. There was no other choice.

He would succeed in claiming his birthright—or die trying.

CHAPTER 3

*E*velyn's back ached as she scrubbed the wooden counters, fighting to keep her eyes open. It had taken her hours to get to sleep; three of the chambermaids had gossiped throughout the night, and the straw of her bed pallet had dug painfully into her skin. She'd briefly fantasized about her plush, twenty-first century king-sized mattress, paired with a fluffy comforter and pillow.

But she'd pushed away the thought. Her mother, as if sensing that Evelyn would one day journey to the past on her own, had taken a young Evelyn on many camping trips and encouraged her natural athleticism. Evelyn had spent countless nights on hard earth in uncomfortable sleeping bags. Sleeping on a hard pallet was something she could get used to, and she'd already observed what life was like in this time.

During her first solo trip to the past, she'd spent

21

a couple of weeks in the year 1382, absorbing the
ins and outs of the fourteenth century, staying in an
inn where she'd told the curious—and suspicious—
innkeeper that she was awaiting her husband.
Attempting to locate her father's family was out of
the question; her mother had told her they'd never
approved of him marrying a Sassenach and had
refused to even acknowledge their marriage.

She'd taken in day-to-day life with awe: peasants tending to their farms, merchants hawking
their wares at the markets, the strange timbre of
their accents. She'd taken in everything she could
about the time period, knowing she'd one day
return. Though she knew she was far better off in
her own time—healthier and better educated—she
couldn't help but wonder what her life would have
been like in this time. Would she be married
already with children of her own? Would she be
the lady of a manor if her father hadn't been
murdered? What would she spend her days doing?

Evelyn took a break from scrubbing, wiping her
brow and forcing her thoughts back to the present.
She just needed to get to the bastard who had killed
her father, Steaphen MacUisdean, and make
certain she hand delivered him a meal doused with
the hemlock she'd brought. After she told him who
she was and watched him succumb to the poison,
she could return to her own time, secure in the
knowledge that she'd destroyed the man who'd
destroyed her parents.

Once the counters gleamed, she dropped her

rag into a small bucket, casting a subtle glance around. She needed to find out where he was in the castle—and learn his schedule. No one had spoken of the laird since she'd arrived; she'd have to get someone to talk. She needed, she grudgingly admitted to herself, to make friends. Preferably with one of the gossipy chambermaids who popped into the kitchens every once in a while.

As if on cue, one such chambermaid, a petite brunette named Aimil, entered the kitchens, her face flush with excitement. Aimil approached one of the kitchens maids, a sour-faced woman named Marsail, as she chopped and prepared a pile of vegetables for a stew.

"I overheard two of the stable boys talking," Aimil told Marsail in a low whisper.

Evelyn lowered to her knees to scrub the floor, her ears pricked.

"Aye?" asked Marsail, not sounding remotely interested.

"Aye. They were saying that Laird Seoras MacUisdean's son has returned—and he's staying somewhere on MacUisdean lands."

"All of the former laird's sons are dead," Marsail returned, still sounding bored. "They've been dead for years. Everyone kens that."

"Not so. They're saying the youngest son— Latharn MacUisdean," Aimil continued, her whispered voice dropping even lower, "was smuggled away when he was a babe. Laird Steaphan assumed the babe was dead; he never kent the lad was alive

23

and went tae his grave thinking so. But somehow, Latharn lived—and now he's back tae claim his title from Laird Padraig."

Marsail snorted. "Yer gossip used tae at least be truthful, Aimil. 'Tis not possible that—"

"Ye both need tae get back tae yer duties," Floraidh interrupted. "There's enough work tae be done without yer gossiping."

Aimil scurried out of the kitchens, and Marsail resumed her chopping, but Evelyn had gone still, her heartbeat thundering so loudly that for a ridiculous moment she wondered if the others could hear it.

Two revelations in under five minutes. Steaphan MacUisdean was dead; his son Padraig had taken over. Latharn MacUisdean, his nephew and the rightful heir—was alive.

She'd tried to find any records on Steaphan MacUisdean during this time frame, but she'd found nothing, coming here on the hope that he was still alive. She thought that she'd feel more regret, more frustration over the fact that he was already dead. But relief swelled within her.

Deep down, she didn't think she was capable of poisoning someone, even if that someone deserved it. Shame roiled through her gut; she'd never told her mother that she planned to kill Steaphen MacUisdean. She could only imagine her mother's disappointment in her had she known. But the knowledge that he was already dead in this time lifted a weight from her shoulders.

Her thoughts shifted to Latharn MacUisdean. His name had come up many times during her mother's stories about the past. Her parents had been friends with Latharn's parents—her father had died in the same coup that had ultimately killed Latharn's parents and forced her mother's return to the present.

Her mother had told her that Latharn, who'd just been a baby at the time, had died along with his older brothers during the coup. If Aimil's words were true, and Latharn was alive and had returned . . .

"What is the matter with my servants today?" Floraidh snapped, pulling Evelyn from her haphazard thoughts. "Why are ye just sitting there like a fool, Eibhlin? Get over here and help prepare the stew."

Evelyn obliged, her mind still racing. As she worked, she recalled the sadness and anger in her mother's voice when she'd spoken of the betrayal of Seoras MacUisdean. If Latharn had come to MacUisdean lands, he could only be here to claim his birthright. Since Steaphan MacUisdean was already dead, perhaps she could avenge her father in a different way—by removing Steaphan's son from power and helping Latharn take his rightful place as laird and chieftain.

She helped one of undercooks sort dried barley into several boiling pots for cooking, her hands shaking as she worked. She needed to find out more information from Aimil. As a chambermaid, she could only guess that Aimil spent most of her time on the upper floors. Evelyn didn't want to risk waiting until night when the other servants were nearby. She needed to get Aimil alone and question her.

But how? She looked around, noticing a male servant struggling with a sack of grain—the same man who'd confronted her when she'd first come to the castle. Taking a deep breath, she approached and helped him lift the sack. He scowled, looking insulted at her assistance.

"I can handle this, lass," he grunted.

"It looks tae me like ye're struggling with it," she returned. She gestured behind her at the busy servants. "The others are busy with their tasks; no one cares that a lassie's helping ye." As he continued to scowl at her, she expelled a sigh. "I can make it look like I'm struggling and ye're helping me—not the other way around—if yer pride willnae allow ye tae accept my help."

The man's lips twitched, and Evelyn could have sworn it was a smile, before it was gone again. He nodded and gave her a grunt of agreement.

Together, they made their way out of the kitchens. Once they deposited the sack of grain in the waiting cart in the courtyard, he muttered his thanks and introduced himself as Tulach.

"There are three more sacks I could use help with," he continued, with a sheepish look.

"I'm happy tae help," Evelyn said with a grin, and this time, Tulach openly returned her smile.

As they carried out another sack of grain, she spotted two broad-shouldered men sweep out of the great hall. A retinue of servants and nobles alike trailed them. She nearly dropped her half of the sack. They were either high-ranking nobles—or Steaphan's sons and heirs, Padraig and Neacal. They were both dark-haired, with the same sharp, angular features.

One of the men, the taller of the two, turned. His eyes met hers, and she froze. His stormy gray eyes were hard as they trailed up and down her body in a way that made her skin crawl. She quickly averted her eyes, continuing down the corridor with Tulach.

When she and Tulach deposited the second sack of grain into the waiting cart, he turned on her with a scowl.

"Ye need tae be careful, lass," Tulach hissed.

"Wh—what?"

"I ken it wasnae yer intention, but ye donnae want tae catch Padraig's eye," he said. "Ye're a bonnie lass. That's all I'll say."

Evelyn stared at him, a slow burning rage filling her gut. Tulach's meaning was clear. His words told her all she needed to know about Steaphan's sons.

Her mother had told her that Seoras MacUisdean showed his servants kindness; hence their loyalty to him. Steaphan's sons had to have learned such behavior from somewhere—their father. Her determination to find Latharn was renewed.

You're not a twenty-first century woman. You're

27

a fourteenth-century humble servant, she reminded herself, as Tulach continued to hold her gaze.

"I'll keep out of his way," she said, forcing herself to look chastened, when she really wanted to tell him that Padraig would be lucky to be alive if he attempted to assault her, given the fight training she'd undergone in her time.

Tulach looked satisfied, and they resumed their tasks. This time, she kept a keen eye out for Aimil, spotting her during their third trip from the kitchens to the courtyard.

"There's a message I need tae pass along tae Aimil. From Floraidh," Evelyn told Tulach, thinking quickly.

Evelyn hurried after Aimil, trailing her into an empty chamber. Aimil whirled, yelping in startled surprise at the sight of Evelyn.

"What are ye doing in here?" Aimil demanded, pressing her hand to her heart. "Ye gave me a fright. Donnae ye work in the kitchens?"

Evelyn swallowed hard and closed the door behind her. She turned back to face Aimil, deciding to get right to the point.

"Aye, I do. I'm here because I need tae ken something. If Latharn MacUisdean is alive and on MacUisdean lands . . . I need ye tae tell me where he is."

EVELYN SAT behind Tulach as they rode away from

the castle on horseback, scowling into the darkness of the sack that he'd unceremoniously placed over her head.

"Did ye need tae cover my head?" she demanded.

"Aye," he snapped. "'Tis bad enough ye ken about Latharn."

Evelyn gritted her teeth. After she'd asked Aimil about Latharn, insisting she wanted to know out of curiosity, Aimil had taken her to the source of the rumor—one of the young stable boys, who'd been in a heated discussion with Tulach when they'd approached.

"I donnae ken where ye heard that rumor," Tulach had answered for the stable boy, shooting the younger man a glare. "Latharn died when he was a babe."

She'd left the stables, defeated and wondering if she should even bother staying in this time, when Tulach had cornered her moments later.

"I need ye tae answer me truthfully," he'd said, eyeing her closely. "Ye didnae just happen tae arrive here at the castle, did ye?"

For a panicked moment, she'd wondered if he knew she was a time traveler, but quickly dismissed the thought as unlikely. She'd decided that she had to take a risk; he might be the only lead to Latharn.

She'd told him who she was and the true reason why she was here—minus the time travel—and Tulach had gone pale. He'd accompanied her to the kitchens without a word, where he'd told Floraidh they were going to run an errand to the village. Once they were alone, he'd thrown a sack over her head, ignoring her protests.

Now, she tightened her grip on his waist, her heart thundering in her chest. Was Tulach truly taking her to see Latharn? Or had she been mistaken in telling Tulach who her father was— and she was walking right into a trap? But then she recalled how Tulach had warned her about Padraig, the sincerity that shone in his eyes. No, she didn't think he was deceiving her—though he'd refused to tell her how he knew of Latharn's whereabouts.

The horse soon slowed, and the sack was removed from her head. She saw that they were approaching a thatch-roofed cottage. A tall red-haired man stood outside of it; he stiffened at their approach. Tulach turned around to give her a sharp look.

"I'll do the talking, lass."

She nodded her agreement, swallowing as he helped her dismount.

"Horas, this is Eibhlin Aingealag O'Brolchan," Tulach said. "Daughter of the late clan noble Tormod Ualan O'Brolchan and Ginnifer Robertson O'Brolchan. They were dear friends with Latharn's parents; Steaphan had her father killed. She approached me at the castle; she wants tae offer Latharn her assistance."

But Horas continued to study her with suspicion.

"There's no one by the name of Latharn here. He died along with his brothers years ago," Horas said, after a long moment. "Now leave. Before I make ye."

Tulach went pale, but Evelyn bristled, sensing that Horas was lying. Latharn was here—or somewhere nearby. She opened her mouth to reply, but another voice cut across the silence. A deep, sexy voice with a distinctive Highland brogue.

"Tis all right, Horas," the voice said. "Let her come inside. I'll at least hear what she has tae say."

Her heart leapt into her throat. Did the voice belong to Latharn MacUisdean?

Horas glared at her, but he stepped aside. Shooting him a glare of her own, Evelyn moved into the cottage, trailing Tulach.

A tall, dark-haired man stood before a hearth, warming his hands. When he turned to face her, her breath caught in her throat.

He stood taller than both of the other men, with a solid, muscular body that was evident beneath the dark tunic and breeches he wore. His hair was raven black and wavy, his whiskey-colored eyes set into a handsome fine-featured face, his angular jaw dotted with a sexy five-o'clock shadow.

This was Latharn MacUisdean, the infant her mother had spoken of? The infant who was very much alive and had grown into the most strikingly handsome man she'd ever seen?

Latharn stepped forward, arching a curious brow as he approached her. Evelyn was always aware of her petite stature, but Latharn made her feel positively miniscule: she barely reached the center of his broad chest.

To her irritation, she could feel her face flame, which she knew made her look ridiculous given her flame-red hair, something her mother and childhood friends had teased her endlessly about, so much so that she always made a conscious effort *not* to blush. She must look like a flustered tomato. A flustered, sweaty tomato in drab servants' clothing. Why hadn't she at least bothered to wash and change into fresh clothes before leaving the castle with Tulach?

Focus Evelyn, she ordered herself. This wasn't a first date. She was here for a serious matter.

"I'm Latharn MacUisdean," the hunky Highlander said, his voice a low burr that wrapped around her like smooth velvet, and she couldn't stop the shiver of delight that ran down her spine. "And who," he continued, his gaze sliding up and down her body, leaving a blazing trail of heat along her skin, "are ye?"

CHAPTER 4

*L*atharn had to force himself to concentrate as the lovely red-haired lass gazed up at him. She was a startling beauty, from her mane of flame-red hair, to her sensual rosebud mouth and proud, high cheekbones with a smattering of freckles. Though she was petite, she didn't lack curves—her plain servant's garb didn't hide the alluring flare of her hips, the tantalizing swell of her breasts . . .

He made himself meet her eyes; her most striking feature. They were amber gold, like the sun come to life. He tried not to stare, tried to keep his expression neutral, even though every one of his senses now hummed with desire.

"I'm Eibhlin Aingealag O'Brolchan," the beauty replied. "My mother spoke a great deal about yer family. I overheard a maid gossiping that ye may be here, so I took a chance and came here with Tulach tae meet with ye. I want tae help ye."

There was something slightly different about her accent, something he couldn't place. He set his preoccupation with her beauty—and her voice—aside as her words settled in, and a flare of irritation arose within his belly. If she'd learned he was here, so could his enemies. He'd have to arrange for new housing as soon as possible.

He turned to Tulach, who seemed to read his thoughts and gave him a nod. Gormal had briefly introduced him to Tulach the day before; he liked the man, he seemed nothing but trustworthy.

"'Tis true. I think it may have been another of Gormal's spies—one of the stable boys who has a loose tongue," Tulach said.

"We'll have tae remove him from the castle," Horas said, his expression hard. "We cannae have loose tongues while ye're in hiding. Gormal can find him a post elsewhere."

Latharn nodded, turning his focus back to Eibhlin.

"Ye want tae help me?" he asked. "Why?"

"Steaphan MacUisdean, yer uncle and the man that killed yer parents, also killed my father," she said, her voice growing hard with anger. "I came here tae kill him—only tae discover that he's already dead. But I can help avenge my father in another way—by removing the traitor's sons from power."

Behind him, Horas let out a skeptical snort, and Latharn shot him a warning look. Aye, she was a petite lassie, but there was a strength to her, a feroc-

ity. He still didn't know how she could help him—
she was a servant. He needed nobles on his side:
strong clan warriors. Not distractingly beautiful
lasses with golden eyes.

"I thank ye for coming here, lass," he said
finally. "And I admire yer courage. But I already
have allies."

Her eyes narrowed, and there was that ferocity
again, burning in her eyes like a violent flame.

"How do ye ken ye'll not need my help?" she
demanded.

"Ye're a servant and a lass," he said gently. "My
plan is dangerous for even the strongest of men. I'm
sorry for what happened tae yer father, but I'll not
have ye coming tae harm—or dying—on my
account."

Her eyes flashed, and she stepped forward.
Her sweet scent filled his nostrils: hints of rosewater and honey. He dragged his gaze from her
tempting, sensual lips to focus on her blazing
eyes.

"And how do ye ken I'll die or come tae harm?"

"I'm sure ye're very capable," Latharn hedged,
trying to keep his voice steady, to not stare at her
inviting mouth. "But I cannae have ye risking yer
life for me."

"I'm not risking my life for ye. I'm doing this for
my father—and my mother. His death destroyed
her, and she never recovered," she said, anguish
flaring in her eyes. "If ye'll not allow me tae help ye
. . . I'll figure out a way tae bring down Padraig on

my own. But ye're making a mistake by not using me."

Giving him one last glare, she turned to leave, but Latharn impulsively stepped forward.

"Wait."

Horas frowned, giving him an imperceptible shake of his head, while Tulach's eyebrows rose in surprise. Latharn ignored them both.

"What would ye do tae help me?"

"I'd spy on the brothers Padraig and Neacal. I can serve meals in the great hall tae listen in on discussions; the head maid prefers lasses tae serve in the great hall. That's something Tulach and yer stable boys cannae do."

She held his eyes, determination shining in the depths of her own. Her offer was tempting; right now, the spies they had were all men. And he knew from his time as a servant that feasts in the great hall was where many important discussions took place—discussions that could give him much needed information about what Padraig was up to.

"Ye'll have tae meet my advisor, Gormal. I'll want him tae ken—and approve—of another spy," he said.

Eibhlin's eyes filled with triumph. She smiled: a wide, luminescent smile that seemed to light her up from within and made her look even lovelier. He made himself shift his gaze to Tulach.

"Can ye both get away from the castle tomorrow around midday?" he asked.

"Aye," Tulach replied

"Tulach will escort ye tae me then," Latharn told Eibhlin.

To his surprise, Eibhlin stepped forward to take his hand, looking at him with intense sincerity. He wasn't prepared for the tsunami of heat that swept over him at her touch.

"Ye'll not regret this, my laird," she said.

She released his hand and slipped out with Tulach. Latharn watched her go as Horas stepped forward with a concerned frown.

"Gormal willnae be happy with this," Horas said. "And, my laird, I say this with respect; I hope ye were thinking in terms of strategy, and not with yer desires, as the lass is bonnie—"

"Ye willnae finish that thought, Horas," Latharn said sharply, glaring at him.

Horas fell silent, offering him a brusque nod before leaving to resume his post outside.

Once he was alone again, Latharn returned his focus to the hearth, studying the leaping flames of the fire. Eibhlin was lovely, aye, but that wasn't why he'd agreed to let her help. In her eyes, he saw the same determination that burned within him to avenge his parents, to take back the titles stolen from him. He could tell that her desire to help was born purely out of love for her deceased father; he'd seen the flare of pain in her eyes when she mentioned him. It was the same pain that shadowed him ever since he'd learned of the circumstances of his birth parents' deaths.

Gormal, Horas, nor any of the men who would

fight for him could understand such pain: such grief tinged with fury. In the few moments he'd spoken with her, he'd seen those emotions play across her lovely features.

And they were lovely features. Even now, his cock lurched in his breeches at the memory of her beauty, of that sinful body hidden away beneath that drab servant's gown.

He gritted his teeth and willed his lustful thoughts away. It would do no good to have such thoughts, especially if she was going to act as a spy for him. He had no time to focus on his baser desires. If he succeeded, he'd need to marry the daughter of a well-connected clan noble to solidify his claim. Later, after he was wed, he could take a mistress if he desired, but he'd not focus on anything—or anyone—else until he'd taken back the titles that belonged to him.

At midday the next day, Latharn paced anxiously in the sitting area of Horas's home.

Gormal decided to move him to Horas's home after he'd learned of his meeting with Eibhlin; it was too risky for him to stay where he could be found. Latharn hadn't wanted to inconvenience Horas by using his home, but Horas insisted that he was never there; he had no wife or children, and he wanted Latharn to use it.

Horas now stood outside, awaiting Tulach and

Eibhlin's arrival, while Gormal sat at the table in the small dining area, sipping a hot broth that Aoife had prepared. Gormal was scowling, still furious over the knowledge that one of his spies' loose tongues had revealed that Latharn was alive—and he was annoyed at the prospect of a lass working for Latharn as a spy. It was only at Latharn's insistence that he'd agreed to at least meet Eibhlin.

Latharn stopped his pacing at the sound of approaching horse hooves. He turned to hurry out, trailed by Gormal.

At the sight of Eibhlin dismounting from her horse, a rush of heat coursed through him. She still wore a drab servant's gown, but this time no coif covered her hair, and her flame-colored locks flowed loosely around her shoulders.

At his side, Gormal went still with shock. Latharn looked down at him, wondering the cause of his reaction. Gormal stepped forward, looking at Eibhlin with such intensity that she shifted uncomfortably beneath his scrutiny.

"When Latharn told me who yer father was, I couldnae believe it," Gormal said, shaking his head. "But ye have his distinctive eyes. Where have ye been all these years? Is yer mother still alive?"

Latharn noticed a brief flash of uncertainty in her eyes before she spoke.

"She died several years back. My mother fled tae the Lowlands after Father died, fearing for both our lives. She had kin who lived on a farm there and they took us in. I grew up there and took work

39

as a servant tae bring in more coin. But I always kent I'd return here tae avenge my father."

"What about yer father's family? Did they not want tae take ye in?"

"They never approved of my father wedding a Sassenach," Eibhlin replied, her mouth twisting with bitterness. "And even though my mother had nothing tae do with what Steaphan did, even though she mourned him for the rest of her life and never took another husband, many of them blamed her for his death. Even if we had gone tae them, they'd have turned us away."

Pain and anger flickered across her lovely face, and sympathy rushed through him. Eibhlin had been through much in her life—and all because of his uncle.

As if sensing his sympathy, she jutted her chin defiantly.

"I donnae tell ye this for yer sympathy. I tell ye this so ye understand why I want tae help."

Before Latharn could respond, Gormal stepped forward.

"I understand wanting tae avenge yer father, but I chose the spies we have at the castle because they're men who escape notice. Ye're bonnie, and those eyes are memorable."

Latharn glowered at Gormal, though deep down he'd had the same thought. How could any man not take notice of such a beauty?

"I'm not the only bonnie lass in the castle," she replied. "As a lass, I can get tae places that yer men cannae. I can handle chambermaid duties and serve in the great hall; the laird prefers lasses as servants there. And ye said it yerself, Latharn. I'm a wee servant lass. No one will suspect me of spying."

Her golden eyes were filled with determination, and pride swelled within his chest. Though he knew that men in the castle would notice her—something which caused him a surprising amount of irritation—she was right about no one suspecting her of being a spy. She looked harmless. A petite, harmless beauty. But by the fiery purpose in her eyes, he suspected that she was as harmless as a poisonous spider.

"I think the lass speaks the truth," Latharn said, offering her a small smile.

"Very well," Gormal grumbled. "But I'll tell ye the same thing I've told the other spies. Even though ye're a lass, if ye get caught, we willnae help ye. The other spies will deny kenning ye."

Latharn wanted to protest, unease coiling around his spine at the thought of Eibhlin being left on her own if she were discovered.

But Eibhlin didn't flinch.

"I wouldnae expect anything else," she said. "I'll do what is necessary tae remove the traitor's sons from power. Anything I can tae help avenge my father and honor his memory."

CHAPTER 5

a tumult of anxiety and desire swirled through Evelyn's body as she rode back to the castle with Tulach. She had to work on hiding her attraction to Latharn. Who would have thought that the baby her mother had spoken of would grow up to become such a—well, a hunk? It had taken everything in her power to not blush and stammer around him. The man was driving her to distraction: his deep, Highland brogue, those whiskey-colored eyes, his defined jaw, that muscular body . . .

She shook her head as if to rid herself of the memory of him. Latharn had the monumental task of reclaiming his titles—and she was his spy. Having erotic thoughts about him would only hinder matters.

"Are ye certain ye want tae do this, lass?" Tulach asked, as they drew closer to the castle.

"Aye," she returned abruptly, her face flaming,

43

as if he could somehow glean that she'd been fantasizing about Latharn.

He turned, shooting her a look that was half skepticism, half admiration, and gave her a nod.

"Ye need tae understand, lass," Tulach said, as they dismounted. "What Gormal said was true. If ye're suspected of being a spy, we cannae protect ye."

"I ken," she said, though her stomach twisted at the thought of what would happen to her if she were caught. She reassured herself that if it came down to it, she could flee back to Tairseach if she ran into danger. But she prayed it wouldn't come to that.

"Tulach, I need ye tae get these barrels of wine down tae the cellar," Floraidh said, as soon as they entered the kitchens. "Eibhlin, help Marsail prepare the stew for tonight's feast."

At the mention of a feast, Evelyn's ears perked up. She needed to serve during tonight's feast—it would be her first real opportunity to spy for Latharn.

Adrenaline fueled her as she worked alongside Marsail to chop a pile of vegetables for venison stew, her mind solely on tonight's feast and how she'd gain useful information. For some reason, she craved Latharn's respect.

Before she knew it, evening had fallen. Floraidh made the female servants, who would serve in the great hall during the feast, wash and change into fresh clothing.

"The laird and the nobles donnae need tae smell ye as they eat," Floraidh said bluntly, wrinkling her nose.

Evelyn's heart pounded against her ribcage as she washed and changed into a fresh servant's gown. Deoridh, the servant whose place she'd taken, had roughly been her size; Floraidh had given her Deoridh's clothing to wear. She hoped she'd find out something useful tonight; Latharn's advisor Gormal and his guard Horas already seemed to think her serving as a spy was a mistake. She needed to prove them wrong.

"I'm sorry about what I told ye—about Latharn being alive," Aimil whispered.

Evelyn whirled, surprised. Aimil hovered behind her with an apologetic smile.

"'Tis all right," Evelyn said. She needed to make certain she seemed loyal to Padraig. "'Tis none of my concern even if he were alive. I'm just happy tae have a post here tae serve Laird MacUisdean."

"The next bit of rumor I share will be truthful," Aimil said with a mischievous smile.

They hurried out of their quarters when Floraidh ordered them to get to work; the nobles were just arriving. Evelyn trailed the other servants to the kitchens where one of the undercooks handed her a platter of fresh bread that she took into the great hall.

Evelyn stifled a gasp as she entered, taking in its grandeur. In her time, the great halls she'd seen in old castles were dank and crumbling, with no hint of the life that had once dwelled within them. This great hall was sprawling and teemed with life; several dozen nobles sat at long oak-paneled tables beneath a high-vaulted ceiling. Candlelight and flames from the roaring fireplace illuminated the hall in a romantic, hazy glow. Fine wool tapestries decorated with nature scenes draped the walls, giving the large hall a homey feel. The tantalizing scent of smoked venison and roasted vegetables glazed with honey hit her nostrils; she couldn't help but inhale.

For a moment, she allowed herself to imagine her parents seated at one of the long tables, their heads bowed close together as they shared a private conversation. Her mother had spoken of meals in the great hall with fondness. At first, she'd found such feasts overwhelming, but as she fell in love with Tormod and the nobles began to accept her, she'd looked forward to the feasts.

Smiling as she thought of her mother, Evelyn set down the platter of bread on one of the tables and took a subtle look around. At the head table sat Padraig, his head bent as a man at his side spoke to him in low tones. On the opposite end of the hall sat Neacal. Neacal looked around the hall with a bored expression, idly sipping his ale. Why wasn't he at the head table with his brother?

As Evelyn swept in and out of the hall for the rest of the feast, setting down and taking away plates, she did her best to listen in on snatches of conversation. But she wasn't catching anything of note, and it was difficult to understand some of the nobles' thick brogues.

She'd started to give up on picking up anything of use when she heard an intriguing snatch of conversation as she walked by the head table.

"It must be done soon tae secure yer claim," the man at Padraig's side said.

"I ken," Padraig said shortly.

"Yer brother doesnae—"

Evelyn had to keep walking to avoid suspicion, but she needed to know more. What must be done soon to secure Padraig's claim? Was his claim not already secure?

When she returned to the kitchens to fetch a fresh pitcher of ale, she decided to be bold. She took a deep breath and returned to the great hall, moving to the head table. She kept her head bowed down low as she refilled cups of ale, listening intently to the conversation.

"And there should be no doubt," Padraig was saying, "my weak brother willnae try anything, but I have him in the castle, under watch, just in case. And as for the others who may try tae—"

Evelyn let out a very modern curse as she accidentally spilled ale onto the table. To her horror, Padraig and the nobles seated next to him stopped speaking. Their eyes all landed on her.

"I—I'm sorry, my laird," she said hastily, wiping at the table with the corner of her apron.

"Look at me, lass," Padraig said, his voice sharp.

Dread swirling in her gut, she looked up at him. He stared at her for a long moment, something unknown flickering in his grey eyes.

"What did ye say? That oath ye swore?"

Evelyn blinked in surprise. And then she remembered that the curse word she'd used—or at least the modern form of the word—didn't yet exist in medieval Scotland. Would telling him the word cause some sort of odd butterfly effect? If she weren't so terrified in that moment, she would have laughed at the thought.

"I—I said, 'fuck,' my laird," she stammered. Of all the conversations she'd imagined having in the fourteenth century, this wasn't one of them.

Padraig raised his eyebrows, amusement dancing in his eyes.

"I've not heard that oath before. I like it," he said, grinning at the nobles next to him. "Where did ye hear such a word, lass?"

"From a Frenchman," she said, thinking quickly.

Padraig and the men around him laughed, with several men jeering about the raunchiness of the French. Evelyn quickly wiped up the ale, hoping that this was the end of it, and she could slip back out the hall unnoticed. But as she started to turn, Padraig's hand went up to grab her arm.

"Take care not tae spill around me again," he bit out. "I donnae like sloppiness, lass."

All humor had vanished from his voice and his expression; his face was completely flat. It was a terrifying transition, and Evelyn now understood how he must use fear to maintain his leadership.

"Aye, my laird," she murmured.

His hand tightened on her arm until she was certain it would leave a bruise. Only then did he release her. Evelyn gave him a hasty bow and left the hall, fear and dread coursing through her.

CHAPTER 6

"Ye didnae hear what he was planning tae do tae secure his claim?" Gormal asked, for what seemed like the millionth time.

Evelyn gritted her teeth. It was the next afternoon; she and Tulach had left the castle to see Latharn under the guise of running an errand to the village. She'd told them what she'd overheard at the feast, deciding to leave out Padraig's notice of her—and his threat. She had no doubt they'd refuse to let her keep spying if they knew what had occurred. And though dread still raced through her veins at the memory of Padraig's cold, cruel expression and his bruising of her arm, she refused to let that one incident dissuade her.

"No. But there will be other feasts I can serve at. I'll be able tae learn more," she said.

"Very well," Latharn said, after a brief pause.

"But be careful. I ken how these feasts can be. Did any of the nobles take notice of ye?"

She swallowed hard. Telling herself the lie was necessary, she shook her head.

"No," she said, and guilt filled her at the relief in Latharn's eyes.

"Do ye both have time for a meal before ye return?" Latharn asked, gesturing to a table behind him.

A strange thrill went through her at Latharn's request, though she told herself he was just being polite. He'd extended the request to both her and Tulach, who looked delighted as his eager gaze landed on the table set with a meal of smoked salmon, bread and ale.

"Aye," Tulach answered for the both of them. "Floraidh doesnae expect us back for some time."

Latharn nodded, but his focus was on her. She felt her face warm under his regard as they all sat down to eat. As Gormal and Horas engaged Tulach in conversation, Latharn sat down next to her.

"I wanted tae thank ye again," he murmured. His breath fanned against her ear, and she had to will herself not to tremble with desire. "For what ye're doing."

"There's no need," she said, keeping her gaze on her plate. "I'm doing this for my parents—and because 'tis the right thing tae do."

"Still," he insisted. "Ye're doing this at great risk tae yerself."

She looked up at him as he offered her a heart-stopping smile, and warmth encircled her belly.

"I heard that ye were a servant for many years?" she asked abruptly, wanting to take the focus off herself—and her lingering guilt over her lie.

"Aye," he said, shaking his head as if he could hardly believe it himself. "Until a few weeks ago, it was all I kent. I did secretly long for more—I was hoping tae elevate my station tae steward one day. I never dreamed that I had a title. Land."

"A title and lands that were taken from ye," she reminded him.

"I ken," he said, giving her a rueful smile. "But 'tis still much tae take on."

"I can only imagine," she said. "I've spent my life as a servant. 'Tis hard for me tae imagine my mother living in a great manor."

Though she wasn't telling the truth about the servant part, she was truthful about her disbelief over her mother living in a fourteenth-century manor. Her mother had seemed so thoroughly modern, with her customary jeans and T-shirts, and the sleek suits she often wore to work. She still couldn't imagine her mother happily wearing medieval gowns. "But I donnae think she cared about the loss of wealth—only my father. Her heart was forever broken by his loss. I always wanted tae fix things for her—tae see her truly happy."

She recalled the lingering sadness that seemed to haunt her mother, a grief that plagued her after being torn from the love of her life and the father of her child. At her insistence, her mother had dated occasionally, but none of the men stuck, and her mother insisted she was fine being alone. But Evelyn knew better. There was simply no one who could replace her father in her mother's heart.

"I'm sorry tae hear about her grief," Latharn said, giving her a look of genuine sympathy. "I do envy that ye at least kent yer mother. I loved my adopted parents, but I wish I could remember my birth parents."

"My mother told me some things about them. Yer mother doted on ye and yer brothers. As did yer father."

She told him more of what she could recall from her mother's stories: how surprisingly athletic his mother had been, performing archery with his father and brothers, accompanying them on hunting trips, not caring about the disapproval of the other nobles. How his father took care to invite a servant to sit at his side during feasts and tell him about his life, encouraging his young brothers to do the same. How both of his parents would never allow the nurses to put him or his brothers to bed; they would insist on singing them to sleep themselves.

Latharn listened to every word, so intently she wished she had more that she could tell him.

"Thank ye, Eibhlin," he said, giving her another heart-stopping smile. "What ye've told me—'tis like ye've given some part of my parents back tae me."

54

"Tell me about yer adopted parents," she said. "What were they like?"

Latharn was silent for a long moment, his eyes filling with both love and melancholy.

"They had many bairns, so they were very strict with us. We had tae tend tae our duties around the house and the land before we could enjoy any leisure. But my father loved tae tell us tales. Tales he'd heard from traveling merchants who visited the lairds he'd served, tales from bards of the clans. And my mother, she liked tae sing as she cooked for us. My father convinced her tae sing for us during our leisure time. She had a lovely voice. Had she been of higher birth, she could have sung at the king's court."

He looked lost in memory for a moment before turning to her.

"And yer mother?" he asked. "She was a Sassenach, aye?"

She hesitated, fearful of giving too much away, but he was looking at her with such genuine curiosity that she relented.

"Aye. She came tae the Highlands tae visit distant kin," she said, sticking with the cover story her mother had used in the past. "My parents' eyes locked at a feast. She said she kent she loved my father the moment she laid eyes on him. She told me he confessed the same tae her. He was the love of her life, 'tis why his death broke her so. She raised me with as much joy and love as she could, but there was always something missing. I just wanted her tae have joy in her life."

A sudden sadness pricked at her chest at the memory.

"I may not have kent yer mother, but I suspect ye did bring her joy."

Her heart picked up its pace at his words and his kind smile, which only made him more handsome. As his eyes locked with hers, a blazing rush of heat spiraled around her belly, and it suddenly became difficult to breathe.

"Eibhlin and Tulach should return tae the castle," Gormal said abruptly, interrupting the moment.

Evelyn tore her eyes away from Latharn's, realizing with embarrassment that the others were looking at her and Latharn. Horas looked curious; Tulach looked amused, while Gormal's face was tight with annoyance.

Evelyn swallowed hard, lowering her gaze. She reminded herself that this was a different time; she was a mere servant, and Latharn would soon claim his title as laird. They were probably breaking all sorts of societal rules by just sitting next to each other.

She got to her feet along with Tulach, giving Latharn a hasty bow.

"Thank ye for the meal, my laird," she said, before turning to leave, her body still tingling with awareness—and unrequited desire.

CHAPTER 7

*L*atharn stood by the door, watching as Eibhlin rode away. Spending time with her had been his only flicker of joy after a trying couple of days.

The day before, Gormal had arranged for him to meet with a noble by the name of Baigh, who'd secretly remained loyal to Latharn's father during the years he'd served Steaphan MacUisdean.

When Latharn had entered Baigh's drawing room, he'd sunk to his knees before Latharn, lowering his head in a reverential nod.

"Yer father remains my chieftain in my heart," he said, shame flickering across his face. "I feigned loyalty tae Steaphan in order tae survive. Ye donnae ken what it was like back then—Steaphan was killing or imprisoning anyone who didnae fall in line. But I always remained loyal tae yer father in my heart."

"Ye donnae have tae apologize," Latharn said,

57

gesturing for Baigh to get to his feet. He'd done nothing to deserve such reverence, at least not yet. He wanted to earn the respect of the men who chose to follow him.

"I'll do what I can—what I must—tae help ye claim yer titles. But I must warn ye, though Padraig has only just come tae power, he's already instilled much fear intae the peasants and clan nobles alike. I fear ye'll have a trying time getting men tae swear fealty tae ye."

A heaviness seeped into Latharn's bones at this, though he'd already suspected this to be true. Baigh offered to bring some of his kin over to his side before Latharn left his home, yet his heaviness had lingered.

"If ye're going tae bed the lass," Gormal said now, pulling him from his thoughts, "do it after ye wed a lass who will help solidify yer claim."

Latharn stiffened, turning to look at Gormal, who was glaring at him. He was grateful that Horas and Aoife were outside—he didn't need them to hear Gormal's words.

"Bed Eibhlin?" he asked, hoping that he looked properly offended, though just the thought sparked a torrent of desire in his belly. Eibhlin lying beneath him, that curtain of fiery red hair spread about, her lovely lips parted as she whimpered his name . . .

"Ye're thinking about bedding the lass right now. Like yer father, ye're not a good liar," Gormal said, his expression softening for a moment, a look

58

of amusement shining in his eyes, before it was gone once more. "The lass is bonnie, aye, but ye need tae think of who ye're going tae wed when ye're laird. 'Tis important that 'tis the right choice; it willnae help yer cause if ye're bedding a servant while we're trying tae secure ye a bride."

"I wasnae thinking of bedding the lass," Latharn lied. "I was just showing her kindness. She's risking her neck by helping me."

"Which is her choice. Put her from yer mind," Gormal ordered with such authority that Latharn bristled. He was tempted to remind Gormal that *he* was the one who would soon be chieftain and laird; he was the one who would dole out orders.

But he opted not to retort, because Gormal was right. He had too much to focus on; his desire for Eibhlin was a distraction.

"I've arranged a meeting for ye with some of Baigh's kin. Baigh thinks he can get them tae agree tae follow ye. If they in turn can get their allies tae follow ye, we can add even more men to our side," Gormal continued. "Then, when ye have enough men, ye can consider allying with Clan Creagach. They've long been allies of Clan MacUisdean, but I ken the chief doesnae care for Padraig. But first ye have tae convince them ye're a worthy leader, which I've no doubt ye can do."

Latharn wasn't as certain of this, but he held his tongue. *I will become a leader my men can admire and respect,* he told himself firmly, pushing his lingering lustful thoughts of Eibhlin aside. *I must.*

~

THE NEXT DAY, Latharn traveled with Gormal and Horas to Baigh's manor, where he was to meet with Baigh's kin: two of his brothers and a cousin. Unlike Baigh's reverential greeting, these men regarded him with skepticism—even traces of suspicion.

"I can see that ye're Seoras MacUisdean's son. Ye have the look of him," Baigh's brother Camron said, eyeing him closely. "But how do we ken ye can lead? Baigh tells us ye've lived as a servant?"

"I ken I'm asking much of ye, tae put yer faith in me. But the blood of my father runs in my veins," he said. He hated to keep bringing his father into this, wanting to win them over to his side on his own merits, but his father's memory was the only asset he had for now. "I promise ye that I will fight for every man who swears himself tae me. I will live for the clan, for 'tis people. 'Tis why I've returned—not for lands, coin or even glory. But tae lead and protect the people who my father loved, who he died for. If I thought Padraig was that leader, I'd have stayed away. But I ken he's not. I need yer help if I'm tae become the leader our clan deserves."

A long silence followed his words. Baigh and Camron looked satisfied by his words, while the others still studied him with uncertainty.

"Give us some time tae talk this over among ourselves," Baigh's cousin Kennen said. "Ye must understand—I donnae bear Padraig no respect. He's vain, petty and needlessly cruel. But he has many on his side on account of his father—though he was a treacherous bastard, he was a decent leader. It will be a great risk tae ourselves and our families if we swear fealty tae another laird."

As he and Gormal returned to Horas's home, he prayed he'd done what he could to convince them.

His anxiety dissipated when he spotted two horses in Horas' stables. He hoped that Eibhlin was here, her presence always calmed him.

He couldn't stop the wide smile that spread across his face at the sight of her as he entered Horas's home. She was seated next to Tulach as Aoife handed them cups of ale. As soon as he entered, they both got to their feet and gave him respectful bows.

He couldn't take his eyes off Eibhlin. Even in the plain brown servant's gown she wore, she was the loveliest lass he'd ever seen. He could only see a portion of her hair beneath her coif; he had to resist the urge to ask her to remove it. He started to greet her, but Gormal stepped forward to address them.

"What information do ye have for us?" he asked brusquely.

"One of the stable boys told me that Padraig had visitors late last night—'tis like he didnae want anyone else tae ken they were coming," Tulach said.

Latharn tore his gaze away from Eibhlin, his body going stiff with dread.

"Who are they?" he asked.

"He didnae recognize them."

"I need ye tae find out who they were," Gormal said. He turned to Eibhlin, and Latharn didn't miss how his expression hardened.

"And have ye learned anything, lass?"

"No," Eibhlin said, her face flaming with shame. "Not yet. But I'm hoping that if I keep listening in during the feasts—"

"We donnae have much time," Gormal interrupted, giving her a look of disapproval. "If ye're not going tae provide us with anything useful, 'tis not worth the risk of having yet another—"

"Ye cannae expect her tae have already learned something, she's just started spying for us," Latharn interrupted, glowering at Gormal. "Give her more time." He turned back to Eibhlin, his tone softening. "I hope ye'll both stay for a meal."

To his delight, they obliged. He knew that he shouldn't sit next to Eibhlin; he kept reminding himself that she was a distraction. But he couldn't stop himself from taking a seat at her side.

"Donnae fret about Gormal," he said in a low voice. "It will take time tae learn anything of import."

She gave him a grateful nod, though her eyes still looked troubled. He wanted nothing more than to put her at ease.

"When I was a servant, my favorite task was tae help clear out the stables," he said, deciding to distract her. "I could only do it when my other duties had been tended tae—and of course there were stable boys tae handle such tasks. The other servants thought it was odd, but I enjoyed it—in spite of the smell. I think I just enjoyed being outdoors."

Her amber eyes widened in surprise, and she chuckled.

"I keep forgetting that ye were a servant," she said, shaking her head.

"I'll never forget," he said earnestly. He'd never forget the years he'd spent toiling as a servant. It was the only work he'd known for most of his life.

"When ye're a servant, ye donnae have much choice in—" he began, before stopping himself. How could he be so forgetful? Eibhlin was a servant—and that was likely all she would ever be. Female servants rarely changed their station in life, often marrying fellow peasants and devoting their lives to their families.

"'Tis all right," she said, as if reading his thoughts.

"Have—have ye wanted tae do anything else?" he asked. "Ye ken yer father was once a clan noble. Did ye not want tae return tae yer former station in life?"

"I was just a babe when he died, so I have no memory of it. Even if I were a noblewoman, I'd not have much choice as tae what tae do with my life. I'd have tae wed and become a mother tae whomever my kin found suitable," she said. "Aye, a servant's life isnae an easy one. But I have some freedom."

Latharn thought of his former laird Artair's new bride, Diana. She was now lady of Artair's manor, and he treated her as an equal partner, giving her leadership duties of her own, ignoring the disapproval of other nobles over such an act. There was also Artair's kin, Niall—his bride Caitria freely indulged in her love of travel and traveled the continent alongside her husband.

"I ken of some noble women who have freedom," he said. "And even though I toiled as a servant, I was never unhappy. Ye make what ye can of yer place in life."

She held his gaze for a long moment, seeming to consider this.

"Roasting meat on the spit," she murmured. "That's my favorite duty. No one else seems tae enjoy it, and 'tis usually handled by young lads, but I take pride in watching the meat roast. I often volunteer tae handle it in the kitchens—and I'm always obliged."

Latharn laughed, and they continued to trade stories of their favorite—and worst—duties they handled as servants.

"I once gambled away a favorite horse of mine during my first post to avoid cleaning out chamber pots," he said, grimacing at the memory. "My parents were furious with me for it, but I was secretly pleased. I've always managed tae avoid that particular duty."

"I hate scrubbing the counters after the butcher has taken out the entrails of an animal," Eibhlin said with a shudder. "I may seem strong, but I grow woozy at the sight of blood."

"Ye're still stronger than most lassies I've met," he told her. "Many men donnae like the sight of blood."

"Ye think much of me, my laird," she said, her amber eyes locking with his.

Latharn returned her teasing smile, his eyes dropping to her sensual lips. He could imagine seizing those lips with his own, of exploring her sweet mouth with his tongue . . .

Tulach's chair scraped as he stood, forcing Latharn's gaze—and lustful thoughts—away.

"I'm afraid 'tis time for us tae return," Tulach said.

Disappointment roiled through him, but he stood with a nod.

He walked them out to the stables, reaching out to help Eibhlin up onto her horse, allowing his hands to linger on the curve of her hips. He ached to pull her delectable body against his, to explore her mouth with his. But, mindful of Tulach's presence, he stymied his desire and turned to walk back toward the cottage. And this time, he didn't allow himself the bittersweet pleasure of watching her ride away.

CHAPTER 8

*E*velyn tossed and turned that night, her thoughts filled with memories of Latharn's soft, velvety laughter, the feel of his strong hands on her body as he lifted her onto her horse, the flare of raw desire in those dark eyes. Her hand drifted to her lips, imagining his tall, muscular body pressed against hers, his lips, hot and demanding, pressed against her own. Arousal spiraled to her center, and she had to resist the urge to touch herself, to imagine Latharn—

Stop it, Evelyn, she chastised herself. That wouldn't—*couldn't*—happen.

She forced her thoughts to less erotic ones. Despite Latharn's assurances, she wanted to find out more information that could help him as soon as possible.

She thought of the gossipy maid, Aimil, who'd told her about Latharn. She could befriend her and find out what else she knew about Padraig and

Neacal. But Evelyn would have to be careful in how she framed her questions and to not arouse suspicion.

She got her chance sooner than she thought, as Aimil poked her head into the kitchens the next morning to request a spare maid to assist her with cleaning the chambers; two other chambermaids had fallen ill.

Evelyn immediately volunteered, and as soon as they were alone, Aimil launched into more of her customary gossip.

"Do ye ken Eion? He works in the buttery. I heard that he's taken one of the clan nobles' daughter tae his bed," Aimil said.

"Aye?" Evelyn asked, feigning interest and intrigue.

As Aimil went into detail about this alleged scandalous love affair, Evelyn waited for her chance.

"Do ye think the laird would care if he found out?" Evelyn asked, when Aimil finally stopped to take a breath.

"I donnae ken," Aimil said with a shrug. "I imagine he doesnae care. He has more important matters tae tend."

"Aye, given that he's so recently become laird," Evelyn said, careful with her choice of words. "What—what do the other servants think of the new laird?"

Aimil fell silent, and her open, friendly expression vanished. Evelyn silently cursed herself. Had she been too obvious?

"Since I'm new tae the castle, I was just wondering if—" she hedged, trying to backtrack.

"We are all grateful tae the laird for providing us with work, protection, and shelter, as we were grateful to the previous laird," Aimil said stiffly. "Finish changing the bedclothes. I'm going tae take the linens down tae wash."

And just like that, Aimil scurried out of the chamber. Evelyn bit her lip, a stab of regret piercing her. She should have warmed Aimil up more and been more careful in wording her inquiry.

But something else disturbed her. Aimil hadn't just looked uneasy—she'd looked fearful. How would she ever learn anything useful if the servants were too fearful to share anything with her? If she could only spy for Latharn by catching snippets of useful conversation in the great hall, she didn't know how much of a help she would be.

"Are ye all right?" Tulach asked, when they were alone a few hours later, hauling a sack of barley flour from the kitchens out to a waiting cart. Aimil had insisted she needed no more help in the chambers, but Evelyn knew better. She'd made a mistake in asking about Padraig.

"I'm not making as much progress as I'd like," she confessed.

"Ye've only just started," Tulach reassured her. "Donnae put so much pressure on yerself, lass."

She gave Tulach a grateful smile. She hadn't known him for long, but she already liked him.

She'd asked him during one of their rides to see Latharn why he was spying for him. He'd only told her it was the right thing to do, but she suspected there was more to it than that. She nodded her agreement, and Tulach disappeared back into the castle.

Evelyn waited until after nightfall to approach Aimil with an apology, when they were both in the servants' quarters preparing for bed.

"I'm sorry, Aimil," she said in a low voice. "About what I asked earlier. I'm new here, and I just wanted tae ken—"

"'Tis fine, Eibhlin," Aimil said quickly. "Donnae speak any more of it."

There was a warning—and fear—in the young woman's eyes.

Evelyn swallowed hard and nodded her agreement. But she knew there was something more to Aimil's words; she just needed to find out what it was.

~

"Ye realize ye may have exposed yerself?" Gormal growled. "That Aimil may mention yer words to others?"

It was the next afternoon, and she had come to see Latharn to inform him about what happened with Aimil. At Gormal's words, Evelyn pulled herself to her full height, meeting his gaze.

"I apologized tae her," Evelyn said. "I told her it was because I'm new—"

"Even more reason tae be suspicious of ye," Gormal snapped. He turned to Latharn. "I told ye it was foolish having her spy for ye."

Latharn didn't acknowledge Gormal's words. His focus was entirely on her, but to her relief he didn't look angry. He looked thoughtful.

"Eibhlin may have helped us," Latharn said slowly.

"How?" she and Gormal asked at the same time.

"I think Aimil kens something. Ye said she seemed more than just fearful—that she warned ye away. And ye say this lass likes tae gossip, aye?" he asked.

"Aye."

"Then keep talking tae her. Befriend her."

"My laird," Gormal said. "'Tis not a—"

"But donnae mention anything about the laird again," Latharn continued, ignoring Gormal. "Engage with her. I think she may open up on her own."

"And how can ye be certain of that?" Gormal demanded.

Latharn stiffened, finally turning his attention to Gormal. Evelyn could detect an undercurrent of tension between the two men.

"I cannae," Latharn returned. "But I have faith in Eibhlin."

A sense of renewed determination swelled within Evelyn at Latharn's trust.

"I'll do what ye suggest," she said.

Latharn smiled at her; it took great effort to not allow a girlish blush to stain her cheeks.

"I'm going tae take my meal outside—'tis rare for us tae have such sun this time of year," he said, gesturing to the sunny day outside. "Would ye like tae join me?"

Gormal's face tightened at this invitation, but Evelyn only saw Latharn and his inviting smile. She agreed, trying not to sound too eager, and they made their way out to the back of the home, where Latharn spread out his cloak for them to sit upon.

Aoife brought them a meal of bread, a savory fish stew and ale. Though the day was brisk, Evelyn only felt warmth as she sat at Latharn's side. She looked around, taking in the vast beauty of the Highlands stretching around them in all its majesty.

"'Tis beautiful here," Evelyn said, taking a bite of her bread, her gaze lingering on the snowcapped mountains in the distance. "I remember feeling overwhelmed by 'tis beauty when I first came here. My mother told me how beautiful it is here, but there's nothing like seeing the Highlands with yer own eyes."

"Aye," Latharn agreed, looking around at the lush scenery. "Though I confess I ken no different; I've spent my life in the Highlands. But I do remember being struck by its beauty when I was a bairn. In those days, my family and I would often share meals like this in between chores," Latharn said, gesturing down at their meal. "We'd eat outside as Father told us tales."

Latharn's face lit up at the memory. Evelyn lowered her bread, hungry for more information about him.

"How many siblings do ye have?"

"Four," Latharn replied. "I'm the eldest. My parents had more of their own after taking me in."

"Do they ken what ye're doing? Who ye are and that ye're taking back yer title?"

"My brother Crisdean does. He's only two years younger than me and we're the closest, but I told him not tae tell the others—they'd only worry or try tae help. They're off living their own lives with families of their own. I donnae want them tae concern themselves with my plight. 'Tis dangerous."

He stared off into the distance, his smile fading and his face shadowing. For the first time, she saw the tremendous strain he must be under; it was plain on his face.

"I ken 'tis not my place tae say," Evelyn said. "But . . . perhaps 'tis not a bad thing tae have yer family with ye . . . tae not have tae take on such a great burden alone."

She braced herself for his ire, for him to tell her to mind her own business, but he just expelled a sigh.

"Ye may be right," he said. "But I donnae want

tae make them a target of Padraig or Neacal. Ye have no siblings, aye?"

"No. My mother never remarried," Evelyn replied, her heart clenching at the memory of her mother's ever-present sadness. "But I understand the urge tae want tae protect them."

Without thinking, she reached out to place a comforting hand over his, and instantly regretted the action, because a firestorm of desire arose within her core. Latharn stilled, his dark eyes clashing with hers.

A heartbeat of silence passed between them. Then another. And then Latharn's mouth was claiming hers; his lips firm and demanding, his tongue exploring her mouth.

Evelyn's heartbeat thundered in her chest, and her senses were aflame as Latharn's hands went around her waist, pressing her closer as he continued to kiss her breath away.

Evelyn had traveled through time. She'd been kissed. She'd even had awkward, mediocre sex. But this kiss—*this kiss*—put every single one of those experiences to shame.

The kiss only lasted for seconds, but it seemed to stretch for several glorious ages. She allowed herself to give in to the need that had spiraled within her ever since she first laid eyes on him. She clung to him as they kissed, suddenly and irrationally never wanting to let him go. She luxuriated in the feel of his muscular body against hers and the firm demand of his mouth. He let out a low, sexy groan against her mouth before he released her.

Evelyn struggled to catch her breath, her eyes wide as they met his. His own dark eyes were smoky with desire as he reached out to take off her coif. Her hair spilled out, falling loosely around her shoulders, and Latharn let out another husky groan that ignited a fire within her belly as he wrapped her hair around his fingers, tugging her face toward his for yet another kiss.

"My laird," Horas said from behind them.

Latharn released her hair and stood. Embarrassment flooded Evelyn as she also stood, readjusting her hair beneath her coif.

If Horas noticed that Latharn was about to kiss her, he gave no indication; his expression remained stoic.

"Gormal wishes tae speak with ye," he said.

Latharn nodded and turned to Eibhlin. Her heart still pounded wildly against her ribcage, and she felt unsteady on her feet, but she moved to step past him.

"I should get back," she said. "Thank ye for the meal, Lath—my laird."

She scurried away from him, her lips—and body—still on fire from his kiss.

CHAPTER 9

*T*he next morning, as Latharn listened to Gormal discuss how to bring more men over to his side, thoughts of a red-haired, golden-eyed beauty kept distracting him. He'd gone to sleep with a painful erection and the memory of Eibhlin's lips against his, her red waves free around her shoulders, their silky strands wrapped around his fingers, her full breasts pressed against his chest, and her tantalizingly sweet smell. He'd imagined her in his bed, his lips pressed against every inch of that soft, delectable skin . . .

"Are ye listening tae me?" Gormal growled. "Ye convinced two of Baigh's kin tae join ye, now we need tae get tae the men loyal tae them."

"I was listening," Latharn lied. He stymied the memory of Eibhlin's lips against his and stood. "I ken we need more men. I've kent that since the day I arrived here."

"I ken of three more nobles who may help,

though I'm not certain where their allegiances lie. But they do have many men loyal tae them, who will come tae yer side if they say so," Gormal said, leaning back in his chair and rubbing his temples. "When ye talk tae them, I think ye shouldnae mention ye were a servant. Perhaps we can say that ye were a warrior for another clan instead. Or even a merchant."

Latharn tensed at this suggestion, though he knew Gormal's suggestion was a sound one. He recalled the dismissive way Baigh's kin had looked at him. He suspected that other nobles would look at him the same way.

Yet he had no desire to lie, to begin his leadership under such treachery. If he did, how was he any different from his snake of an uncle?

He stood to approach the hearth, gazing down into the flames. How to win over the nobles?

Ye donnae. The thought struck him with the force of a speeding arrow.

Perhaps he was focusing on the wrong people— the nobles. Perhaps he should focus on the common people, the people who toiled the lands, the servants. The common people outnumbered the nobles. What if he could secure their loyalty, using his past as a servant to his benefit?

He whirled to face Gormal, voicing aloud his thoughts, but Gormal scowled.

"The nobles donnae care what the peasants think," he said, waving his hand in dismissal. "'Tis the nobles who will ultimately swear fealty tae ye.

'Tis their fealty ye need tae become chief and laird."

"Aye. But if their own servants and the peasants who toil their lands express their loyalty tae me, it may very well sway them," Latharn insisted. "How many nobles or lairds ken what 'tis like tae toil? My past can help me get the common folk over tae my side."

"'Tis still a risk," Gormal grumbled, after a long pause. "The common folk may not care—they tend tae not get involved in disputes among the highborn. But if this is what ye want tae do . . ."

"Aye," Latharn said firmly.

"Then we can start with the servants of Baigh's household," Gormal said, still looking reluctant. "They're more loyal tae Baigh than tae Padraig."

The tension ebbed from Latharn's shoulders. Despite Gormal's reluctance, his heart told him this was the way forward.

He stiffened at the sound of horse hooves approaching outside. He frowned; Eibhlin and Tulach weren't supposed to arrive until later.

"Stay here," Gormal ordered, his hand going to the dagger he carried in a sheath at his side as he strode toward the front door. But Latharn didn't heed his order, following him outside.

Horas stood several yards in front of the door, his body tense, his sword drawn. Latharn reached for the sword at his side as a cloaked figure approached on horseback.

"Stay where ye are!" Horas shouted, as the rider came within earshot.

The rider obliged, reaching up to lower the hood of his cloak. Latharn froze, both unease and relief flooding him as he took in the rider's familiar face.

"My laird—" Horas protested, as Latharn strode by him to approach the rider.

"Crisdean," Latharn snapped, taking in his younger brother. "What are ye doing here?"

HOURS LATER, Latharn stood opposite Crisdean, glaring at him. He'd had Gormal send Crisdean a letter informing him of his new location at Horas's home, but he'd again warned him to stay away; he didn't want any of his family members in danger. But his stubborn brother had ignored his wishes and informed his other siblings of his true identity as the MacUisdean heir—and what he was doing here. Fortunately, Crisdean had convinced them to stay away and let him help Latharn.

Latharn had spent most of the afternoon trying to convince him to leave, telling him how dangerous it was for him to help. But Crisdean steadfastly refused, insisting that he wouldn't leave Latharn to fight on his own.

"Ye can warn me of the dangers all ye want, brother," Crisdean said calmly, leaning his large body back in his chair and pinning him with his dark eyes. "But I'll not leave ye tae handle something this dangerous on yer own. It only took me this long tae join ye as I had tae make certain my farm is looked after while I'm gone. And," he added, with a mischievous wink, "when ye're laird, I want ye tae gift me lands and coin."

"I cannae grant ye lands if ye die on my behalf," Latharn returned through gritted teeth.

"I donnae have any intention of dying," Crisdean said, unflinchingly calm. "Ye'll not scare me away, Latharn. I'm staying."

Latharn expelled a sigh, closing his eyes. Crisdean had looked up to him when they were younger, eager to go riding and hunting with him when they'd completed their chores. But it was one thing to want to tag along with him when they were still bairns—to fight with him was another thing altogether.

"It will be good tae have another man tae fight for ye, my laird," Gormal said from behind him.

Latharn tensed; he should have known that Gormal would be of no help. He looked at Horas, who gave him a nod of agreement.

"Gormal is right. Yer brother wants tae help," Horas added.

Crisdean gave him a smug look, arching his eyebrow as if daring him to keep protesting. Latharn let out another sigh; there would be no dissuading him.

"I'll have a bed pallet for ye placed in my room," he said grudgingly.

Crisdean grinned, and in spite of himself, Latharn softened. Though he was still concerned for Crisdean's safety, it would be good to have a familiar face around.

Crisdean's gaze shifted to something behind Latharn and his eyes widened with interest.

"Who is the bonnie lass?"

He turned. Through the open doorway he could see Eibhlin and Tulach dismounting from their horses. A sudden, sharp stab of jealousy spiraled in his gut as he noticed the way Crisdean was eyeing her. Crisdean had always been popular with the lassies; many had fallen to his charms. He'd told Latharn on more than one occasion that he enjoyed variety too much to settle for one lass.

"She's not for ye tae bed," Latharn said, unable to keep the growl from his voice. "She's working for me as an ally—spying on the current laird."

Crisdean nodded, but he still trained his gaze on Eibhlin in a way he didn't like.

Latharn reluctantly introduced Eibhlin and Tulach to Crisdean. Eibhlin looked startled as she took in Crisdean; he knew she was thinking of their last conversation when he'd insisted on keeping his siblings out of his plight.

"I just learned that there's tae be a gathering at the castle tomorrow," Eibhlin informed him, once the introductions had been made.

"What sort of gathering?" Gormal demanded.

"We donnae yet ken, but I think it may involve only the clan nobles," Tulach said.

"I'll make certain tae serve in the great hall again," Eibhlin said, a look of fierce determination spreading across her face. "I'll find out what I can."

"Let's pray ye learn something useful this time," Gormal said coolly.

Latharn shot him a glare, but Eibhlin didn't even flinch at Gormal's words.

"I'll do everything I can to find out something of use," she said.

Horas, Tulach and Gormal dispersed, speaking in hushed tones by the hearth, as Latharn sat down for a meal with Crisdean and Eibhlin. He noticed with annoyance that Crisdean sat down next to Eibhlin, his eyes roaming appreciatively over her body.

"Do ye not need tae rest from yer journey?" he asked Crisdean, irritated.

"No. I'm well rested," Crisdean said, not taking his eyes off Eibhlin. "Tell me, lass, does yer husband approve of yer spying? 'Tis a dangerous job for a lassie."

"I have no husband," Eibhlin replied, her lips twitching in a smile; she seemed very aware of Crisdean's flirtations.

"And why is that? A lass as lovely as yerself—"

"Crisdean," Latharn interrupted, his brother's name coming out in another growl. "I told ye tae leave Eibhlin be."

"I was just asking her a question," Crisdean said innocently. "Unless ye have a claim on the lass?"

83

"No," he said, though the protest sounded like a lie, as Eibhlin said, "No one has a claim on me."

An abrupt silence fell. He met Evelyn's eyes, wanting to challenger her. *Ye were all mine when I had my lips on yers,* he wanted to say. But, aware of Crisdean's keen eyes on them, he kept silent, though a treacherous part of him wanted to loudly declare that Eibhlin was indeed his.

"My apologies," Crisdean said, raising his hands up. "I didnae mean tae offend ye, lass."

"'Tis all right," Eibhlin replied, giving him a small smile. Latharn couldn't help scowling; he didn't like Eibhlin gifting her lovely smiles to his brother.

"Now 'tis only fair that ye ask me a question," Crisdean said, returning her smile.

Eibhlin set down her bread, cocking her head to the side as she slid a mischievous look toward Latharn.

"All right," she said. "Tell me. How was Latharn as a lad?"

Surprise—and embarrassment—coursed through Latharn, along with a trickle of male pride that she'd asked a question about him and not his brother.

"He was a wee thing: reed thin and unable tae hold his own in a fight," Crisdean said.

"'Tis not true," Latharn grumbled, though this was very true, and both Crisdean and Eibhlin laughed.

He watched as Eibhlin leaned forward,

listening intently as Crisdean regaled her with stories about their childhood—the pranks he and his brothers would pull on each other, how their parents would lovingly scold them, how they made each other laugh, even during the long days of performing their chores. For a few moments, he allowed himself to relax as he traded jests with his brother, enjoying the genuine delight on Eibhlin's face as they talked.

The meal was over all too soon, and regret pierced him when it was time for Tulach and Eibhlin to leave. He insisted on walking Eibhlin to her horse, and when they reached it, she turned to him with a wide smile.

"Yer brother is a jovial man," she said. "But I'm surprised ye allowed him tae help ye."

"I didnae," Latharn said. "My brother is very stubborn."

"'Tis because he loves ye," she said, a look of envy flickering across her face. "Ye're fortunate tae have siblings now that yer parents are gone."

"Aye," he said, glancing back at the door where Crisdean stood, watching them. "I ken. Eibhlin," he added, stepping closer and lowering his voice. It took great effort to not gaze at that luscious mouth of hers, to not claim it again with his own, but he held himself back. "Be careful at tomorrow's feast. Donnae bring any attention tae yerself."

Hesitation flickered in her eyes, but she gave him a hasty nod. He wanted to question her more, to discern that reluctance, but she was already mounting her horse. He helped her the rest of the way up, allowing his hands to again linger on the flare of her hips, stepping back as she rode away.

Crisdean approached as he watched Eibhlin and Tulach ride off into the distance, lowering his voice.

"Be honest with me, brother," Crisdean murmured. "Are ye bedding the lass?"

"No," Latharn replied, glaring at his brother. *But I want tae. Desperately.* "Even though I'm not, stay away from her. She needs tae focus; she doesnae need yer flirtations."

"The lass didnae even notice me," Crisdean said. "Did ye not notice how she hungered for stories about ye? If ye havenae bedded her yet, I ken she'd happily spread her—"

He had his hands on the collar of his brother's tunic before he could finish his sentence.

"Donnae speak of Eibhlin that way. She's bonnie, aye, but she's risking her life tae help me. None of my men—not even ye—will bed her. She's under my protection."

To his annoyance, his brother didn't look threatened, only amused. Latharn released his grip on Crisdean, who cocked an eyebrow.

"For someone who isnae bedding the lass, ye act as if she's yers."

"Crisdean—"

"I'll not say any more," his brother said, throwing up his hands in a gesture of surrender.

"But ye should ken . . . even though ye'll soon have a title, life doesnae have tae be all about duty."

Crisdean gave Eibhlin's retreating form a meaningful look before he turned to head back inside.

CHAPTER 10

"Out of bed with ye, lass!"

Evelyn awoke with a start. She looked around in mortification as she realized she was the only one still in bed in the servants' quarters. Servants in this time awoke well before dawn, and she'd become used to the schedule. But last night she'd lain awake well into the night, flush with giddiness over the meal she'd shared with Latharn and his brother.

Floraidh stood next to her bed, scowling down at her, her hands on her hips, as Evelyn scrambled to her feet.

"I donnae ken where ye went last night, and I donnae care, but if ye start sleeping past the others, I'll have tae—" Floraidh began.

"I'm sorry, Floraidh," Evelyn said quickly, hoping that she didn't press and demand where she'd gone. But Floraidh was already heading out of the quarters, grumbling about the duties she needed to handle before tonight's feast.

Evelyn threw herself into her duties, her thoughts returning to the previous evening. She'd enjoyed herself more than she'd anticipated, hanging onto every word as Latharn and his brother shared stories of their childhood. Even though she knew some facts about Latharn on a surface level, she didn't realize how starved she was for more information about him. She recalled with a smile how he'd laughed and joked along with Crisdean, how relaxed and happy he'd looked. She'd felt the same, and during the meal, she was able to forget that she was from another time with an important duty to carry out. She'd allowed herself to just . . . *be*. Shecouldn't recall a time when she'd felt so content and happy.

"Will ye be serving at the feast tonight?"

She blinked, emerging from her reverie. She was chopping a pile of onions for a stew and her knife nearly slipped. Tulach stood before her, clutching a sack of barley flour.

"I'll make certain of it," she said, embarrassed that she'd been so immersed in thoughts of Latharn. *You're here for a purpose, not to have date nights with Latharn,* she scolded herself.

Tulach looked satisfied and wished her luck before leaving. She hadn't considered what her strategy was for tonight's feast, but there wasn't much she could do other than pray that a noble let something of importance slip. She'd just have to be extremely careful to not get herself noticed like she had last time.

As she helped one of the undercooks glaze some roasted vegetables with honey, she kept her ears perked, hoping to learn any details about tonight's gathering, but the servants kept their chatter only to the tasks at hand. Even Aimil, who pointedly avoided her gaze when she came into the kitchens, didn't have a word of gossip to share.

By the time evening fell, exhaustion had seeped into her bones from working on her feet all day, but adrenaline kept her alert. She needed to pay attention to every single detail that she could pass along to Latharn.

When she entered the great hall with platters of fresh bread and roasted vegetables, nobles packed every inch of the hall. They were all dressed in their finery: dark wool tunics and belted plaid kilts, the deep rumble of their voices punctuated by laughter and jests. Evelyn kept her head down and drifted to the side tables, her eyes sweeping around the hall until she spotted the two brothers. Again, she noted that Padraig and Neacal sat far apart; Padraig at the head table, Neacal at one of the side tables.

She set down the platters of food before several nobles, ignoring the appreciative glances they cast her way. As she walked back out of the hall, passing Neacal's table, she heard a snatch of conversation that made her want to pause, but she forced herself to keep walking.

"Not all accept young Padraig as chief and laird. The longer ye delay—"

Evelyn left the great hall, her heart hammering. Latharn already knew that not all accepted Padraig as laird and chieftain. She needed more.

As the evening progressed, she tried to pick up more information, lingering as she refilled cups of ale and removed and replaced plates of food, but she heard nothing of particular significance; the nobles were now discussing their favorite horses and who was the best hunter among them.

Evelyn's mouth twitched; her mother had told her that men in medieval times weren't far removed from men in modern times.

"Replace sports with hunting and cars with horses," her mother had told her with a wry smile. "And they have the same interests."

The nobles were becoming drunker with ale, which she hoped would loosen tongues. But one of the unfortunate side effects of their drunkenness included them eyeing her and the other female servants a little too much.

"What's yer name, lass?" asked one drunken noble, a pudgy man with bushy eyebrows and intense dark eyes, as she refilled his cup.

"Eibhlin," she said, turning to hurry away, but he reached up to clamp his hand around her wrist.

"Eibhlin," he repeated, slurring her name as his gaze raked appreciatively over her form. "How about ye join me when I return tae my guest chamber for the night?"

92

Panic spiraled through her; she had the feeling he wasn't asking her; it was a demand. She gritted her teeth, trying to resist her modern-woman urge to dump the pitcher of ale she carried over his head.

"Leave the lass be, Oilbhreis," a gruff voice ordered from the opposite end of the table. "There are plenty of whores in the village for ye tae enjoy. Leave the castle servants alone."

She looked up in surprise. Neacal was glaring at Oilbhreis, and the older man obliged, releasing her wrist. Neacal's eyes slid to hers; she quickly turned away, not wanting him to take any further notice of her.

To her great relief, a skirmish broke out at the head of the hall, and both Neacal and Oilbhreis turned to face the commotion, giving her the opportunity to scramble away.

"Ye ken the rightful heirs were yer cousins! The cousins yer father had murdered!" a clan noble roared.

Evelyn stilled, turning to face the head table. Two guards rushed forward to approach the angry noble. He looked to be in his early sixties, with graying, blond hair and blue eyes, though his face had a youthful intensity as he glared at Padraig.

Evelyn's eyes slid to Neacal. He made no move to intervene and defend his brother—nor his late father. He remained seated, his eyes trained on his brother without a hint of emotion.

Padraig, however, had leapt to his feet, his hand on the hilt of his sword.

"Speak another word and I'll have yer head, Dunaidh!"

"I donnae care what ye do tae me—not anymore," Dunaidh roared. "Ye've nothing but greed in yer heart. Ye're no laird of mine!"

"Get him out of here! Put him in the dungeons!" Padraig hissed.

The guards obliged, grabbing Dunaidh by his arms and dragging him from the hall.

"Does anyone else have anything tae say?" Padraig challenged, whirling to face the other nobles. She noticed that Padraig's gaze seemed to linger on his brother. But Neacal didn't move a muscle, his expression remaining stoic as he evenly met his brother's gaze.

The rest of the nobles fell silent; many of them had gone pale with fear.

"I donnae take treachery lightly," Padraig said, his voice carrying to every corner of the hall. "Hear this—if there are any more traitors among the clan, I will find ye. And when I do, I willnae show ye mercy."

Latharn, Gormal, and Crisdean listened intently as Evelyn described in detail what happened at the feast last night.

It was the next day; Evelyn had counted the seconds until she could leave the castle to tell Latharn what she'd learned at last night's feast.

Tulach couldn't join her; a shipment of grain had arrived at the castle and he had to spend the day hauling it down to the storerooms, but he insisted that she come alone—last night's events were too important not to share right away.

There was a long pause as she finished. Latharn's expression went tight; he turned to Gormal.

"Do ye recognize the name?" he asked.

"Aye," Gormal said, shaking his head in disbelief. "Ailbeart Dunaidh. He was close tae yer father, but I didnae ken he was still loyal tae him. He never breathed a word against yer uncle."

"Ye said they put him in the dungeons?" Latharn asked, turning back to face her.

"Aye," Evelyn said. "Padraig was enraged."

"We need tae get him out," Latharn said. "If he's loyal tae my father, he'll join me."

"Agreed," Crisdean said with a firm nod.

"I donnae advise that, my laird," Gormal said.

"Ye ken what Padraig is capable of. He'll put Dunaidh tae death tae make an example of him," Latharn growled.

"It was his choice to speak out at the feast," Gormal said. "And a foolish one. Ye donnae have enough men yet tae risk an assault on the castle."

Evelyn could almost taste the tension between the two men as a long silence stretched. Latharn glared at Gormal, but when he spoke, he addressed Horas, who hovered behind him.

"Horas, do ye ken any guards at the dungeons—any who will accept bribes?"

"Aye," Horas replied.

"I want ye and two men ye trust tae go tae MacUisdean Castle and bribe them tae release Dunaidh. I'll give ye some coin. If they ask who sent ye, just tell them it was one of Dunaidh's men," Latharn said.

Pride swelled within Evelyn at Latharn's defiance of Gormal; she personally thought the older man was too imperious with Latharn. Gormal's mouth tightened, but he said nothing.

"Aye, my laird," Horas said, and she could have sworn she saw a look of pride in the guard's eyes as well.

"Thank ye for telling us this, Eibhlin," Latharn said, turning back to her. "I ken ye have tae get back. Let me walk ye tae yer horse."

When they reached the stables, Latharn reached for her hand, turning her to face him, and that familiar awareness corkscrewed its way through her body at his touch.

"I've been a servant at feasts of drunken clan nobles," Latharn murmured, his handsome face creased with concern. "Did—did anyone touch ye? Say anything inappropriate?"

She thought of the drunken noble's proposition and Neacal stopping him, and Padraig's threat at the previous feast, swallowing hard. Now would be the time to tell him about both instances. But she didn't want to say anything that would make Latharn stop using her as a spy.

"Aye," she finally admitted, deciding not to

divulge any more detail. "But it was nothing. I can handle myself, Latharn."

Anger flared in Latharn's eyes. His mouth tightened, and he raked a hand through his dark hair, the gesture making his hair sexily tousled. She averted her gaze. Why did Latharn have to be so distractingly handsome?

"I donnae want ye tae come tae any harm," he said. "Perhaps—perhaps ye've done enough tae help me and—"

"No," Evelyn swiftly returned. "I want tae help until ye've earned yer titles back and the traitor's son no longer rules the clan. I told ye—'tis the best way tae avenge my father."

"I think yer father would have wanted yer safety above everything else," he challenged. "But I ken how determined ye are." He smiled down at her, and something flared in his eyes. Longing? Desire? "My father told me and my siblings tales of beasts who stalk faraway lands, called lions, some with golden eyes like yers. Ye remind me of what a female one would be like. A lioness."

His voice grew husky, and the simmering need in Evelyn's gut flared into desire. Her mouth went dry, and she found her body moving closer to Latharn, almost of its own accord.

"Eibhlin," he whispered. She ached to tell him her true, modern name, just to hear it on his lips. *Evelyn*. "Lioness."

He snaked his hand in her hair, pulling it back so that his eyes clashed with hers. He leaned in, claiming her mouth with his, thoroughly plundering it with his tongue. Evelyn let out a whimper as the kiss deepened, as he explored every inch of her mouth. Her heartbeat thundered as her body strained against his, and he pressed her against the wall, his arousal prominent against her abdomen. Evelyn sucked in her breath and let out a moan.

When they broke apart, his lips trailed along her jaw, down to her throat, and she again arched her body toward his.

"God, how I want ye," he whispered.

"And I ye," she returned, her voice catching on another moan as he reached out to tilt her head back, nipping hungrily at the base of her throat.

"I should say that we shouldnae kiss anymore," Latharn murmured, pulling her close, his lips against her hair. "But I cannae stop, lass. I've never wanted a lass as I want ye."

Evelyn's heart soared as he pulled back, gazing into her eyes with such searing intensity that her breath hitched. For a few taut moments, she considered telling him the truth; it hovered on her lips.

Latharn seemed to sense this, studying her with a frown.

"What is it, Eibhlin?"

Evelyn tried not to flinch at the name—the name her mother had given her in the past. But how would he react if she told him she was born in the past but lived in the future? Even her father hadn't believed her mother was a time traveler when she'd first told him; she'd had to tell him of several future events until he did—and her father had loved her mother. Latharn desired her, but desire wasn't enough for him to believe such an insane story. She imagined his kind eyes blazing with fury and disbelief before sending her away. A powerful wave of hurt swept over her at the thought.

"I think that we should put distance between us." She forced the words past her lips, her stomach clenching at the hurt that flared in his eyes. "I—I donnae want tae distract ye from yer duty. I ken ye must marry a noble lass tae secure yer claim. It will only impede ye tae dispense amorous attentions on a servant like myself. We shouldnae be alone together anymore."

CHAPTER 11

*E*ibhlin was hiding something from him—
something besides her painful words of
keeping her distance from him. He could tell that
some confession had hovered on those lovely lips
after he'd kissed her, before she'd shut herself off
and insisted they no longer be alone together.

The thought plagued him long after she'd
ridden away, her face pale and closed off, lingering
even as he discussed Ailbeart Dunaidh's rescue
with Horas. Horas was friendly with two guards at
the castle whom he could bribe for access to the
dungeons. For his safety, Latharn would have to
stay behind during the rescue, something he hated
to do, but Gormal insisted that if he fell into
Padraig's hands before they had enough men to
defend him, it would mean his doom.

After the discussion over Ailbeart's rescue
came to an end, he rode to another village tavern

along with his brother and Horas to convince a group of local farmers to fight for his cause.

"I ken what 'tis like tae have a poor harvest, tae not ken when yer next meal will come," he said, when some of the farmers reacted with skepticism. "I've heard of the current laird's cruelty. He doesnae care about the common folk who toils his land. I do—because I've been ye. I am ye. And ye have my word, on my father's honor, that I will defend ye with my life, that ye will never starve when I'm laird and chieftain."

When the meeting concluded, most of the men had pledged their allegiance to him.

"Ye did well in there, brother," Crisdean said, as they left the tavern and made their way to the horses.

Latharn just gave his brother an abrupt nod. He knew he should feel pleased, but he still had many more men to convince, and time was running out. It wouldn't be long before word spread to Padraig that Latharn was alive and determined to reclaim his titles. He needed to be prepared before that happened.

His thoughts strayed to Eibhlin and the mystery of whatever she was hiding. He didn't suspect her of treachery or betraying his cause; he only saw sincerity in her eyes when she spoke of defeating Padraig and restoring Latharn to his rightful place as head of the clan. No, it was something else that she was hiding. He was determined to find out exactly what it was.

"My laird."

In the middle of the night, just after he'd fallen into a fitful sleep, he awoke to the sound of Horas' voice. He sat up abruptly; Horas stood at the doorway.

"We've rescued Ailbeart Dunaidh—I had the help of two guards who hate Padraig and who've agreed tae help us," Horas said, beaming. "I barely had tae bribe them."

Relief flooded Latharn; he'd feared they wouldn't be able to rescue Ailbeart in time.

When he left his bedroom, he found Ailbeart standing before the hearth, along with Crisdean and Gormal. Ailbeart's face was bruised, his skin pale, but at the sight of Latharn, a tumult of joy flickered across his face.

"Ye have the look of yer father," he breathed, shaking his head. "I didnae truly believe ye were still alive. I—I apologize for serving yer uncle. Yer father was a good man—a great one. I—"

Latharn held up his hand. He didn't need Ailbeart to echo the same words Baigh had uttered when he'd promised to serve him.

"All is in the past," he said.

"Ye have my allegiance, Latharn MacUisdean. I will do what I can tae help restore ye tae yer rightful place as laird and chief," Ailbeart swore.

"I thank ye for joining me," Latharn said, holding his gaze. "But the first thing ye need tae do is apologize tae Padraig—on yer knees. Tell him yer men rescued ye from the dungeons, but ye've been humbled by yer time there and ye've realized the error of yer words."

Everyone in the room looked at him in startled surprise. Gormal opened his mouth to speak, but Latharn again held up his hand for silence.

"I need ye close tae Padraig—I need tae ken what he's planning," Latharn said firmly.

A look of hesitation flickered across Ailbeart's face. It was a dangerous thing he was asking Ailbeart to do, but it was necessary. If Padraig was as prideful as he suspected, he would take Ailbeart back into his circle—as long as Ailbeart fell to his knees before him.

After several long moments, Ailbeart gave him a nod.

"It will be done, my laird," he said.

"But," Latharn continued, "if necessary, ye can disavow all knowledge of my presence here. We'll have a man on ye tae make certain no harm comes tae ye—and tae ensure he doesnae imprison ye again."

"I'll do all that ye ask, but I'll not disavow ye," Ailbeart said, shaking his head. "I once turned my back on a good man—yer father. I'll not do it again."

During the course of the next fortnight, Ailbeart joined the small but growing group of men who'd pledged their loyalty to him. He learned that Padraig planned to again raise rents on the tenants of the lands, even after a difficult winter when the poorest had little to spare. This had sparked Ailbeart's outburst at the feast, the outburst that Eibhlin overheard.

Ailbeart, along with Tulach, Eibhlin and two other castle workers, now informed him of what Padraig was up to. He also learned that Padraig was insecure about his status as laird; he was seeking to wed a noblewoman who would solidify his claim and he was also making the nobles swear oaths of fealty to him—again. That explained the late-night visitors one of the stable boys had seen come to the castle.

Padraig's brother Neacal, however, didn't seem concerned with either helping Padraig secure the lairdship or taking it away from him. He tended to his own manor and men, only visiting the castle for feasts.

"I still donnae trust him," Gormal said. "I think we need tae keep eyes on him."

Latharn agreed, and they had the guards Horas was friendly with take periodic rides out to Neacal's manor to see if he was up to a coup of his own, but they saw nothing that caused suspicion.

Most of this information came from Ailbeart, who proved to be such a useful ally that Gormal apologized to Latharn for not wanting to rescue him from the dungeons. Eibhlin could only inform them of which nobles visited the castle, and the nobles discussed nothing more of note at the feasts. Even though she had the least amount of information to share, it was her visits he looked forward to the most.

Yet she kept to her word and remained distant and closed off, keeping her visits brief, only offering clipped responses to his questions and declining to stay for meals with them. He soon grew weary of this; though he desired her fiercely, he missed more than just her lips on his—he missed their talks. Her companionship.

"Tulach informed me Floraidh doesnae expect ye back for some time," he said, when she arrived to inform him about an upcoming feast one sunny midday, after days of her continued distance. "Will ye take a brief ride with me?"

Her golden eyes filled with surprise as they locked with his, and she opened her mouth with what he knew was a protest.

Gormal, Crisdean and Horas were seated at the table behind them, and he doubted they could hear, but he made certain to keep his voice low as he stepped forward.

"I promise tae not touch ye, lass," he whispered, giving her a teasing smile. "I miss yer companion-ship, that's all."

That was a lie. He missed her lush body pressed against his, the sweetness of her kisses, but he didn't want her to put more distance between them.

Eibhlin gave him a shy smile and a hesitant nod, and relief washed over him.

Latharn ignored the pleased look from Crisdean and the disapproving look from Gormal as he informed them that he and Eibhlin were going for a ride.

Horas accompanied them as they rode away, but he seemed to sense Latharn's desire to be alone with Eibhlin, keeping his distance and riding a dozen yards behind them.

The air was brisk and heavy with the promise of rain as they rode, though the sky was a clear and bright blue. The weather in the Highlands changed as rapidly as the flutter of a hummingbird's wings; he hoped it stayed dry long enough for him to have time alone with Eibhlin. He didn't want her to use a downpour as an excuse to flee back to the castle right away.

But the weather held, and they soon reached a loch that sparkled beneath the midday sun, surrounded by lush green trees and edged by white sandy banks. They silently took in the loch's beauty for a moment before watering their horses and tying them to a nearby tree. Latharn didn't see Horas, but knew he was nearby. He was thankful that Horas had given him and Eibhlin privacy; his perceptive guard must know how much he desired her.

"Gormal told me that my birth parents liked tae come tae this loch together and walk along its banks," he said, taking in its glistening waters. "Now I see why. 'Tis peaceful."

He could see the lingering reticence on Eibhlin's face vanish. She smiled, turning to face the loch.

"Aye, my mother told me she and my father would sometimes join them," she said.

"And ye?" he asked. Eibhlin rarely talked about herself—she mostly spoke of her mother. "Were there any lochs near yer home where ye liked tae visit as a bairn?"

The lightness in her face vanished, and Eibhlin stiffened.

"No," she said shortly. "There were always chores tae tend tae."

"I had chores in the fields and at home," Latharn pressed. "But I was still able tae visit the nearby forest."

Eibhlin fell silent for a long moment, her gaze trained on the loch's waters.

"I liked tae take long walks," she said finally. "There was a hiki—a path tae walk along near our cottage. Sometimes I'd go with my mother, but most of the time I'd go on my own. I . . . I liked tae do things many lassies donnae enjoy—or arenae allowed tae do."

"Aye?" he asked, intrigued.

"Aye. I . . . I enjoyed training in archery, sword fighting, and horse riding," she said. "Perhaps 'tis because I am what many consider wee. Training tae do such physical things has always made me feel stronger."

He looked at her in quiet astonishment. How could her mother afford for her to take such lessons, such lessons that only nobles and the wealthy could afford? Perhaps her mother kept some coin when she fled.

But his senses again told him she was hiding something; something was missing from her story. She seemed to sense his growing suspicion, abruptly turning away from him.

"We should get back," she said, but he reached out to stop her.

"Eibhlin . . . I want ye tae ken ye can trust me," he said, holding her gaze.

She flinched, removing her arm from his. But he stepped closer, ignoring the stab of desire that pierced him at their proximity.

"When ye're ready tae tell me whatever it is ye're hiding . . . I'll be ready tae listen."

CHAPTER 12

When ye're ready tae tell me whatever it is ye're hiding . . . I'll be ready tae listen.

Latharn's words echoed in Evelyn's mind as she lay in her straw bed that night. If only he knew what she was hiding. *I was born in 1364 to a time-traveling American and a Highland noble. I lived in the twenty-first century before returning to this time via a magical ancient village.* She had to bite her lip to stifle a bitter laugh, imagining the look on Latharn's face if she told him the truth.

She'd tried to keep her distance from him, but she'd found herself . . . missing him. When he'd taken her to the loch, she'd wanted to open up to him more, to tell him about herself—her *true* self. And she'd ached for him, longing for him to kiss her again. Desperately.

"Who is he?"

Evelyn started as she looked over at Aimil, who

lay in the straw bed next to hers. She had turned to face Eibhlin, eyeing her with a playful smile. Surprise roiled through her; Aimil had been avoiding her ever since she'd tried to pry her for information. While she was glad Aimil was talking to her, she didn't want to discuss Latharn.

"What?" Evelyn asked, stalling. "I'm not thinking of a man."

Aimil arched a skeptical brow, leaning forward, keeping her own tone low.

"I saw the same thing happen with Deoridh, the lass ye replaced. She'd leave the castle for long stretches of time and then return with a foolish look on her face like the one ye're wearing now. I'll ask ye again. Who is this secret lover of yers?"

Panic flared in Evelyn's chest. She'd thought— hoped—the errands she ran for Floraidh had masked her absences. Had anyone else noticed her long departures from the castle? She swallowed hard, thinking fast.

"He's not my lover," she replied, deciding to stick to an old adage. *When lying, stick as close to the truth as possible.*

"But there is a he?" Aimil asked, her eyes twinkling.

"Aye. There's someone I—care for," she hedged. "I donnae want tae tell ye exactly who he is . . . but he's a servant. We cannae be together. He's pledged tae marry someone else."

Evelyn was proud of herself for the hastily put-together lie, yet as Aimil gave her a look of genuine sympathy, a sliver of guilt creeped through her.

"I'm sorry tae hear," Aimil murmured. "But that doesnae mean ye cannae enjoy him before he weds. Ye're a bonnie lass, I'm certain he willnae refuse ye. I can make excuses for ye if ye need tae sneak out and meet him. I have herbs that will prevent ye from getting with child."

Evelyn stared at her, astonished. Yes, she had known it was likely that people in this time—especially servants—didn't behave like the puritans history books portrayed them as. Her mother had told her of a few sex scandals among the lowborn and highborn alike. *Sex is sex no matter what century*, her mother had told her. Yet to have someone in this time encourage her to not only make love to Latharn, but to practice safe sex, seemed so incongruously modern. It was just a reminder that even though she was hundreds of years in the past, people hadn't changed much.

Aimil grinned, misconstruing her look of shock.

"I ken ye're new here, but surely ye've worked in the household of a noble before? Many of the servants—married or no—have lovers." Her expression suddenly darkened. "And Laird MacUisdean has a taste for—"

Aimil abruptly stopped herself. Evelyn watched her, praying she would say more, but Aimil's sudden shuttered expression was like watching a door slam shut. Again.

"That's all the advice I have," Aimil said,

letting out an exaggerated yawn and turning away from her.

Evelyn remained awake, hanging on to the carrot that Aimil had dangled before her. She was certain that Aimil's full statement was, "The laird has a taste for the servants."

She recalled his hand on her arm with a shudder and Tulach's warning when she started working at the castle. *Ye donnae want tae catch Padraig's eye. Ye're a bonnie lass. That's all I'll say.*

Which servant was Padraig bedding? Was Aimil one of them?

The next morning, Aimil was back to her friendly, chatty self, as if her distance of the past few days had never happened. But when Eibhlin tried to get her to elaborate on her words about Padraig, she just waved away her words and told her she knew nothing of the laird's bedmates.

She reported Aimil's words to Latharn and Gormal the next afternoon, but she didn't get the reaction she'd hoped for.

"We already kent that," Gormal said with a scowl. "He likes lassies, lowborn and highborn alike. As did his father before him. I'm surprised he hasnae yet tried tae take ye tae his bed. Perhaps . . ." Gormal said, studying her closely, as if seeing her for the first time, and dread twisted its way down her spine. Was Gormal suggesting that she sleep with Padraig? Just the thought made her skin crawl.

Latharn let out a snarl, and Evelyn whirled toward him, startled. Latharn's hands were clenched at his sides, his face flaming with fury as he glowered at Gormal.

"I donnae ever want tae hear ye make such a suggestion again," he growled. "Ye didnae want her tae spy for me because she's bonnie. And now ye suggest she whore herself for the bastard?"

"My laird," Gormal said, his voice contrite, though his expression didn't match his tone, "what better way for the lass tae get—"

"No," Latharn interrupted, advancing toward Gormal, whom he towered over, and Evelyn now noticed a trickle of fear in the older man's eyes. "She stays clear of him. Ailbeart is keeping a close watch on Padraig for us. There's no need for Eibhlin tae become his whore."

Gormal gave him a nod of acquiescence, going slightly pale. Latharn turned his focus to her, and Evelyn had to actively tap down the swell of warmth that arose within her at the rage that still burned in his eyes. A part of her wanted his reaction to be born of jealousy, but she told herself he was just being protective.

"Donnae heed a word he said," Latharn murmured, as Gormal stepped away. "Padraig doesnae speak of his lovers with the other nobles; he willnae tell Ailbeart such things. Find out what ye can, but ye keep out of his path."

He growled the last part of his order, and a burning arousal crept between her thighs.

"Aye," she whispered, fighting against the force of her desire for him. "Understood."

~

A PAINFUL ACHE throbbed between Evelyn's thighs as she returned to the castle and tried to focus on her duties. Her thoughts were torn between Latharn's sexiness and ways to coax more information from Aimil—but as always, thoughts of Latharn won out. Why couldn't he have been short, balding and pudgy? Perhaps then she would be a better spy and not struggle with him distracting her. Her face warmed as she thought of his anger when Gormal hinted that she sleep with Padraig; a shameful part of her still wanted his furious reaction to be born out of jealousy.

Her thoughts were so wrapped up in Latharn that she didn't notice a man approach her as she made her way down the corridor toward the kitchens.

When she did notice, it was too late to avoid him.

Neacal strode toward her, and she realized with growing horror that he wasn't just walking down the corridor—he was purposefully moving toward *her*. He didn't stop until he stood before her, gazing down into her eyes.

Panic flooded every part of her body. She ducked her head low and murmured, "If ye will pardon me, my—"

"Yer eyes," Neacal said, reaching out to grab her chin and tilting it up to meet his eyes. Dread seared her chest; her heart began to hammer against her rib cage. "I noticed them at the feast, and now I ken why ye look familiar. They're yer father's eyes."

It was suddenly hard to breathe. If he recognized her as her father's daughter—now a traitor as far as the clan was concerned—he could hand her over to Padraig.

She swallowed, trying to figure out what to say, how to get out of this, as he took her arm and maneuvered her into an empty chamber, his eyes still pinned on hers.

"My father had yer father killed," he said, matter-of-factly. "He was named as a traitor of Clan MacUisdean. Why did ye return tae the place of his murder?"

There was no harshness in his question, only genuine curiosity. She took a breath, wishing she could lie about her identity—but she couldn't. Her damned eyes had given her away, something she should have anticipated.

"Lass?" he pressed.

"After—after my father's death, my mother and I fled tae the Lowlands," she whispered. "By the time my mother died, there was no money. I had a hard time getting work, so I returned tae where I kent my parents once lived, hoping someone would take pity on me and offer me a post. I took another servant girl's place. If ye want me tae leave—"

"No," Neacal said, stepping back with a frown. "Ye donnae have tae leave. But there are rumors that Latharn MacUisdean is alive and has returned tae these lands tae reclaim his title. Do ye ken anything about this?"

You know nothing, Evelyn told herself, as her panic swelled. She schooled her expression into one of disbelief. She needed to give an Oscar-worthy performance on the spot.

""'Tis impossible," she breathed. "The former laird's sons are long dead."

He held her gaze for a long moment; she knew he was searching for a hint of deception. She kept her eyes wide, praying that she looked genuinely astonished.

"Very well, lass," he said finally, and relief swirled through her. "But 'tis best ye avoid my brother's notice. Stick tae the kitchens if ye must."

"Aye, my laird. I thank ye," she said, dipping into a hasty bow before hurrying away from him, though she felt his burning, intense eyes follow her as she fled.

CHAPTER 13

*W*hen Eibhlin entered Horas's home, her skin was pale, and panic shadowed her eyes.

Latharn immediately shot to his feet at the sight of her. He'd been in discussion with Crisdean and Gormal about the number of fighting men Padraig had on his side, but as soon as he saw Eibhlin's face, the discussion was forgotten. He strode across the room to approach her.

"What happened?" he asked, fury racing through his veins. Had someone harmed her?

"Neacal recognized me," Eibhlin whispered. "He—he warned me tae stay out of sight. He also told me there are rumors about yer return. He seemed tae believe me when I told him I ken nothing about it."

Dread flooded Latharn's body while behind him, Gormal swore an oath.

He'd known that word would eventually get to

Padraig that he was alive and on MacUisdean lands once he started recruiting commoners to his cause. But the rumors of his return didn't concern him; he was only worried for Eibhlin.

"Ye shouldnae return tae the castle," he said. "That wasnae a warning. It was a threat."

"Latharn, he could have taken me tae Padraig right there. Instead, he let me go. He even seemed . . . concerned," Eibhlin murmured, looking deep in thought.

"That was tae make ye feel secure," Latharn returned. "Have ye forgotten what a treacherous snake his father was? Ye can no longer stay there. Ye need tae leave, tae get far from these lands."

His heart twisted as he said the words, but he had to put her safety above his desire for her.

Hurt flickered in her eyes before it was replaced by determination, the same determination he'd seen on her face the first time they met.

"What do ye ken about Neacal?" she asked.

"Why does that matter?" he snapped.

"Because I donnae think he's like his brother," she said. "I've watched him at feasts. He doesnae seem tae like being there. He doesnae seem anything like Padraig. He's . . . quieter. Almost . . . kind. A noble propositioned me at a feast, and Neacal ordered him tae leave me be. When Tulach warned me about Padraig liking the lassies, he didnae mention Neacal. I think—"

"Eibhlin," he bit out, "they were both raised by the man who murdered our fathers. They—"

"Padraig may be like his father, but I donnae think Neacal is," Eibhlin protested. "If he were, I wouldnae be standing here right now."

"I think Eibhlin is right," Crisdean interjected. Gormal and Crisdean now hovered behind him. "Neacal could have just taken her tae the laird."

"That proves nothing," Latharn hissed. "For all we ken, he could have told his brother ye were there, and they're waiting for ye tae return. Or he could have had ye followed."

"I took a different route here and stopped periodically tae make certain I wasnae followed," Eibhlin said. "Latharn . . . it may be possible that Neacal doesnae care for leadership. What if he could be an ally? What if he could help ye?"

Latharn just looked at her in horrified disbelief. To defend Neacal was one matter. But to suggest that he work with his enemy as an ally was madness.

"Padraig and Neacal were in conflict over who would take the lairdship," Latharn said, through gritted teeth. "If Neacal didnae want that—"

"But how do ye ken for certain?" Eibhlin asked. "What if—"

Latharn held up his hand for her silence. He turned to Crisdean and Gormal.

"Leave us." He barked the words. "I want tae talk tae Eibhlin alone."

His brother frowned and looked like he would protest, but at the furious look on Latharn's face, he obliged. Gormal, he noted, looked pleased that he

121

was angry with Eibhlin. He gave Latharn a respectful nod and swept out of the home with Crisdean.

When he turned back to Eibhlin, he noted that she'd gone pale again, but she'd also pulled herself to her full height, steadily holding his gaze. He stalked toward her, trying to control his anger—and his burgeoning jealousy.

"What," he snapped, "exactly happened between the two of ye?"

The defiance vanished from her eyes, and they widened.

"What?" she gasped. "Ye mean—between me and Neacal?"

"Aye," he demanded. "Ye come here and tell me that ye believe Neacal is trustworthy and that he could be an ally. How did he convince ye of this, lass?"

Eibhlin's disbelief turned into rage. She moved toward him until they stood toe-to-toe.

"How dare ye?" she hissed. "He didnae touch me, if that's what ye're suggesting. I'm telling ye this based on what I've observed about the man. And I donnae ken for certain if he can be an ally, 'tis just something I suspect may be the—"

"Neacal is our enemy," he barked. "If ye donnae understand that, perhaps ye should no longer serve as a spy, and go on yer way."

"I can still spy on my own," she snapped.

"Is that for certain, lass? I could have my men

remove ye from the castle, and send ye away by force."

He hated using his power—power he was just becoming acquainted with—over her, but he was determined to keep her safe from harm, and to remove the ridiculous notion that Neacal could be his ally from her mind. He'd never forgive himself if anything happened to her.

"Very well, *my laird*," she said stiffly, putting an emphasis on his title. "I'll keep my distance from Neacal."

She started to move past him, but he reached for her hand, pulling her close.

"Eibhlin," he murmured, his tone softening. "Ye must ken I care for ye. I just want tae protect ye. Donnae forget that Neacal is the son of Steaphan MacUisdean. If ye insist on returning tae the castle, I want ye tae only stay for a fortnight. 'Tis a risk for ye tae stay any longer now that Neacal kens who ye are."

Eibhlin swallowed, but she gave him a jerky nod.

"Aye," she murmured. "But—at least think over what I said. Talk tae yer other spies, and see what they have tae say about Neacal."

"All right," he grumbled, though he knew he would do no such thing. He would never work with the son of the man who'd destroyed his family. "As long as ye stay away from Neacal."

She gave him another jerky nod, trying to step

back from him. But he couldn't help himself; he pulled her even closer and claimed her mouth with his. For a moment, she stiffened before melting into his kiss, wrapping her arms around his neck with a soft sigh as he plundered her mouth. He held her close as he peppered kisses down the side of her jaw, the long arch of her throat, down to her luscious bosom.

"Latharn," she murmured on a moan. He ached to lower the bodice of her dress, to seize one of her rosy nipples into his mouth, but he feared he wouldn't be able to stop himself from making love to her if he did.

"There's not a man alive who doesnae want tae do that—who wants tae do more than that," he whispered, reluctantly releasing her as he stepped back. "Ye are the loveliest lass I've ever seen; I ken I'm not the only one who has noticed ye. So ye stay out of his path—and the path of other nobles. Or consequences be damned, I'll march intae that castle and haul ye out myself."

HE FOUND it difficult to concentrate after Eibhlin left; he was still worried about Neacal knowing who she was. What if she returned to a trap, and Padraig and Neacal raped her—before murdering her? What if—

"The lass is strong," Crisdean murmured, sensing his worry for Eibhlin. "She'll be fine.

Tulach and the other spies willnae let anything happen tae her."

He gritted his teeth, wanting to tell his brother that he should be the one to protect her, not his men. But he only offered his brother a curt nod.

"I think ye should consider what the lass said about Neacal," Crisdean said tentatively, but Latharn shot him a glare.

"No. I willnae ally myself with my enemy."

"I agree with Latharn," Gormal said. "Neacal remains our enemy—I donnae trust him."

Crisdean's mouth tightened, and it looked as if he wanted to say more. Instead, he got to his feet.

"I need tae take in air," he said, turning to leave the home.

"My laird," Gormal said, once Crisdean had left them.

"Aye?" he asked absently, rubbing his temples, his thoughts already returning to Eibhlin.

"I ken ye care for the lass. That ye desire her."

Latharn tensed, but there was no use denying the truth of Gormal's words.

"But . . . as we gather more men, ye need tae think of yer actions as laird. A laird needs a lady, a suitable one. I think now's the time tae make an alliance with the clan I told ye about—Clan Creagach. I ken there are many suitable lassies in the clan ye can consider as yer bride."

Latharn remained stoic, though unease now encircled his gut at the thought of taking a bride. Eibhlin's face flickered in his mind.

"If they kent that ye'd be willing tae secure an alliance with marriage, I believe they'll join us," Gormal continued. He trained a look on Latharn. For the first time it wasn't an imperious one, but a look of genuine pleading. "I believe ye can be a great leader, my laird. But great leaders must make sacrifices for their people, putting them above all others. Even the ones they care for."

CHAPTER 14

*E*velyn hacked at the pile of carrots with her knife, torn between remnant anger and desire. Her mouth still burned from Latharn's kiss, yet frustration and fury over his dismissal seared her insides. Did Latharn not trust her enough to even consider her suggestion about Neacal?

She had to remind herself that she was a mere servant in this time, no matter who her father was. And Latharn did consult with her far more than other lairds would with commoners. She could even understand his hesitation over considering Neacal as a potential ally. But his complete dismissal still hurt.

You can still find out Neacal's true allegiance on your own, she told herself.

"Eibhlin, can ye help me in the master chamber?" Aimil asked, poking her head into the kitchens and forcing Evelyn from her tumultuous thoughts.

Evelyn blinked at her in surprise, though she shouldn't have been. Aimil had done a complete one eighty from her previous caginess and now talked her ear off whenever they were alone, as long as Eibhlin didn't bring up Padraig. Evelyn wondered if she could subtly find out more about Neacal from Aimil. If she did, she'd have to be very careful. She now knew that Aimil could shut herself off at the drop of a hat.

"Aye," she said, handing the platter of chopped carrots to one of the undercooks and accompanying Aimil out of the kitchens to one of the bedchambers.

For several long moments they worked in silence, working together to change the bedclothes until Aimil paused, giving her a long look.

"Aye?" Evelyn asked.

"Ye have tae tell me what had ye so angered that ye were slaughtering those poor carrots," Aimil said, her eyes twinkling with amusement.

Evelyn returned her focus to the bedclothes, biting her lip. *You need her on your side,* she reminded herself. *You have to give her something.*

"I'm upset with the man I care for," she said finally.

"Aye?" Aimil asked, her eyebrows raising the way it did whenever she shared—or learned of—a bit of juicy gossip.

"Aye. I feel he doesnae respect me," Evelyn

continued. "I gave him my advice on—on something concerning his family, yet he didnae want tae take it."

"Men are stubborn," Aimil said, studying her closely. "What advice was it?"

Dread coiled around Evelyn's body, and she stiffened. Was she imagining things, or was Aimil prying a little too much?

"Just a private family matter," she said, with a dismissive wave of her hand.

Aimil dropped the bedclothes and rounded the bed, taking both of her hands.

"Ye can tell me anything," she said. "I may enjoy gossip, but I ken when tae keep a secret."

Aimil held her gaze for a long moment, and Evelyn's unease flared. Could Aimil suspect she was hiding more than just a secret lover?

But Evelyn pushed aside her unease; Aimil was just prying for more gossip.

"I ken," Evelyn said, with a polite smile.

"And donnae let that stubborn lover of yers cause ye grief," Aimil continued, with a rueful smile. "I ken how stubborn men can be."

"Is there a stubborn man ye care for?" Evelyn asked, returning her smile.

Aimil didn't respond for such a long moment that Evelyn feared she'd again crossed some unknown line. To her surprise, Aimil's eyes began to glisten with tears.

"There is someone," Aimil whispered.

"Someone I care for deeply. Someone I'd do anything for."

A deep pain shadowed Aimil's eyes, and a stab of guilt pierced Evelyn. She'd dismissed Aimil as a flighty gossip, but she could now see that Aimil was carrying a great deal of anguish.

"Ye can tell me as much or as little as ye want about him," Evelyn said gently.

Aimil's expression tightened, and regret flickered across her face.

"Eibhlin," Aimil began. "I—"

She looked at Evelyn, a cacophony of emotions playing across her face, before her expression shuttered and she looked away.

"Make certain tae take these bedclothes down tae the laundress. I'm going tae start on the other chamber," Aimil muttered, still not looking at her as she scurried out of the chamber.

Evelyn watched her go, frowning. Aimil had been on the verge of telling her something. But what? She bit her lip, considering going after her, but decided against it. Demanding to know what Aimil was hiding would only make her shut down more.

She was careful to give Aimil her space during the next few days, only helping her in the chambers when she asked and responding to her questions without asking any of her own. Aimil went back to her gossip, never showing a hint of the pain she'd revealed to her, and Evelyn felt she was right back where she'd started with Aimil. Nowhere.

As for spying on Neacal, she wasn't making any progress on learning anything more about him; no one mentioned him and he no longer visited the castle, not even for feasts.

At Latharn's insistence, she continued to visit Horas's home every couple of days to check in. But she had nothing new to report; she suspected he just wanted to make certain she stayed away from Neacal.

During her visits, Latharn was noticeably distant and never asked her to stay for meals. It was as if the kisses they'd shared, and his confession of caring about her had never happened. His distance mirrored how she'd tried to avoid him after their kiss days before.

This is for the best, she told herself, after one such meeting during which he'd barely looked at her. She'd spent most of her time talking to the sour-faced Gormal instead. *Nothing can ever happen between the two of you.*

But still, she missed him. Missed the way his face lit up with a smile, how nostalgia entered his eyes when he spoke of his parents, even the angry determination in his expression when he spoke of Padraig. And if she were truly being honest with herself, she missed the feel of his lips on hers.

After a week of his distance, she volunteered to stay for a meal, hoping he didn't turn her away.

"Ye should head back," Latharn said dismissively. "If ye're hungry, I'll have Aoife prepare ye something."

She left with bread from a sympathetic-looking Aoife, who seemed to sense the tension between her and Latharn.

She blinked back tears as she mounted her horse: Latharn's rejection stinging her heart. What was she still doing here? She wasn't making any progress, and she'd promised Latharn she would leave the castle in another week. She had no doubt that he would carry out his threat to have her removed. If she wasn't making any progress, there was no reason to stay in this time. She'd have to return to the present, having failed to fulfill her goal, filled with longing for a man who lived in the past.

She decided to take a bold step if she was going to make any progress. Neacal was never in the castle, and she feared scaring Aimil off by inquiring after him. She had nothing to lose—it was time to take a risk.

When there was a break in her chores, she made her way up to the top floors of the castle toward a chamber she assumed was Padraig's study, she'd seen many nobles come in and out of it. She'd avoided it, not wanting to fall into Padraig's line of sight. But now she slipped into the adjacent chamber, pretending to dust, while listening closely to what was happening in the next room.

For a while there was only silence, and she feared that too much time would pass, and she'd have to return to the kitchens. But she soon heard

132

footsteps approach the chamber and two voices—
one of which she recognized as Padraig's.

"Tulach and two other men are being held in
the prisons," she heard Padraig say. "There may be
others—we're still looking. My brother is away; now
is the time tae locate any who may lurk."

Evelyn froze, fear and panic tearing through
her.

"So 'tis true? Latharn MacUisdean is alive and
intends tae take the castle?" the other man asked.

She couldn't hear Padraig's response as they
closed the door behind them. Evelyn's hands began
to shake, and she dropped her rag, reeling from
what she'd just learned. Tulach and two other men
imprisoned. And it sounded like Latharn's presence was no longer rumor—they knew he was alive.

Panic propelled her out of the chamber. She
needed to get to Latharn, to warn him before it was
too late, to tell him about Tulach and the others.

As she hurried down the corridor toward the
stairs, she nearly collided with Aimil, who emerged
from the stairwell.

"I am sorry about this, Eibhlin," Aimil said, her
eyes full of genuine regret. "Truly I am."

"What are ye—" Evelyn began, but Aimil
reached out to grip her arm, focusing on something
behind her.

"I have the spy, my laird," Aimil said.

Icy fear coursed through her veins. Aimil's grip
remained firm on her arm as she turned to face
Padraig, who approached from the opposite end of

the corridor, his lips curled back in an enraged sneer.

When he reached her, he grabbed her by the hair, yanking her head back with such force that she felt several hairs tear from her scalp. She bit her lip to stifle a cry of pain as Padraig leaned in close, until he was only a hairbreadth away from her face.

"Eibhlin Aingealag O'Brolchan. Daughter of the traitor Tormod Ualan O'Brolchan and his Sassenach bitch. Ye will regret the moment ye stepped inside my castle, ye treacherous whore."

CHAPTER 15

"*M*y laird!" Latharn whirled as Horas entered, his eyes wild.

He was standing with Crisdean before the hearth, a cup of ale in his hand. He nearly dropped his cup at the look of panic on Horas' face. He'd never seen his stoic guard look so alarmed.

"Padraig has discovered ye're here. He has Tulach, Eibhlin and yer other spies imprisoned. We need tae get ye off these lands."

Latharn moved to the door, his brother on his heels. He'd only heard one word from Horas's lips. *Eibhlin.* Terror and frustration collided in his chest; why had he allowed her to return to the castle? He should have insisted that she not go back, her protests be damned.

"I'm going after her and my men," he said.

"I'm coming with ye, brother," Crisdean said,

clamping his hand on his shoulder, and Latharn gave his brother a look of gratitude.

"Aye," Horas said, but he hurried to stand before Latharn and Crisdean, blocking their exit. "But not now. First, we have tae get ye off these lands before Padraig sends his men here tae kill ye. I'm a good fighter, but not good enough to fight off a group of men on my own."

"I'll not leave Eibhlin and the others—"

"I ken," Horas said, "but they'll all be lost if ye're dead. We first need tae get ye off these lands, and then we'll rescue Eibhlin and the others with the men who've pledged themselves tae ye. The longer we delay now, the longer it will take tae rescue them."

Latharn swallowed hard, his frustration swelling as he gripped the hilt of his sword. He hated it, but he knew Horas spoke the truth.

Latharn and Crisdean trailed Horas off MacUisdean lands on horseback; he had to force himself to not turn his horse around and race back to the castle. He tried not to think of what Padraig could be doing to Eibhlin right now. Red-hot fury rippled through him at the thought of Padraig laying a hand on her.

Ye will rescue Eibhlin and yer men, he swore to himself. *Ye will get her back. And ye will murder Padraig with yer bare hands.*

They rode until they reached a manor house in lands just beyond MacUisdean lands, the lands of

Clan Creagach. Though Clan Creagach were allies of Clan MacUisdean, Horas assured him he was safe here for now. The manor belonged to a trusted friend and ally of Baigh's who was currently away in England.

When he entered, he was both surprised and relieved to see over a dozen of his men gathered, along with Gormal.

"I sent word tae them as soon as I learned what happened at the castle," Horas said, answering his silent question.

"I thank ye for coming," Latharn said, giving the men a grateful nod. "Ye ken that Padraig has my men—and a lass—who have been spying on my behalf. They're servants and common folk who work the land, just like ye. I'll not leave them tae suffer at Padraig's hands. I pledged as yer future laird tae not let any harm come tae any men who swear themselves tae me."

"I grieve for those who've been captured, my laird," Gormal said, stepping forward. "But they are beyond our help now. They all kent the risk of spying for ye. Now that we're in the lands of Clan Creagach, ye need tae forge a direct alliance with them. They can supply men tae help ye defeat Padraig."

Latharn looked at Gormal in disbelief.

"Ye want me tae leave my men—and Eibhlin—in Padraig's hands?"

"Ye will have tae make many difficult decisions

as laird," Gormal replied, his expression as cold and implacable as a slab of stone. "This is one of them."

Fury swelled within him. In a practical sense, Gormal was right. Padraig's men still vastly outnumbered his, and he needed to focus on the larger battle to come.

But Latharn couldn't leave Eibhlin and the others to die by Padraig's hand. He wouldn't.

"As laird and chieftain, *I* will be the one tae make such decisions. I'll not leave those who fight for me tae die—the same way I wouldnae let any of ye die," he said, turning to face his men. "'Tis a great risk, aye. If any of ye donnae wish tae help, ye donnae have tae."

He waited for any man to leave, but to his relief, his men stood their ground, keeping their determined gazes trained on him. He turned to Gormal, whose eyes flashed with anger. But he said no more words of protest.

He turned his focus back to his men. "Let's rescue our allies."

I'm coming for ye, Eibhlin.

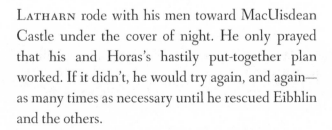

Latharn rode with his men toward MacUisdean Castle under the cover of night. He only prayed that his and Horas's hastily put-together plan worked. If it didn't, he would try again, and again—as many times as necessary until he rescued Eibhlin and the others.

He adjusted his cloak; he wore a hooded one that disguised his features. Another one of his men, of similar height and build, rode at the head of the group. He was acting as a decoy; if they were captured, he would pretend to be Latharn. Latharn didn't like this plan, not wanting anyone to die on his behalf, but Horas, Gormal, and even his brother had insisted.

He glanced over at his brother, who rode alongside him, his gaze trained fixedly ahead. Pride arose in his chest; his adopted parents would have been proud of the brave, loyal man their son had become. As if sensing his thoughts, Crisdean slid a glance toward him and gave him a nod.

Latharn turned his gaze to the lands ahead as he saw the stone turreted towers of a castle looming ahead, and something twisted inside him. Longing? Grief? He'd only seen MacUisdean Castle from a distance; it was odd that this magnificent fortress was the place of his birth and his by right. And at this very moment, the woman he cared for was being held prisoner there. Determination swept over him; he kicked the sides of his horse to make him gallop faster.

As they drew closer to MacUisdean Castle, he gave a nod to several of his men, who rode their horses toward the stables as he and the other men rode around to the back of the castle where the dungeons were.

Since they were severely outnumbered, they planned to use a distraction. And the best distraction was fire. While a group of his men set fire to a portion of the stables, he and his other men would get into the dungeons with the help of the guards who'd pledged to help Latharn.

His pulse thrummed erratically at the base of his throat as they made their way to the rear of the castle. He waited anxiously until he heard the roar of flames and shouts of alarm from the stables.

He gave his men a nod, and they charged toward the rear of the castle, swords drawn.

One of the guards loyal to him waited for them there, giving them an encouraging nod as he swung open the back gate. But the guard abruptly stiffened, and horror roiled through Latharn as a sword pierced him straight through from behind. The guard slumped forward, dead.

Another guard stood behind him, removing his bloody sword from the guard's dead body and charging toward them with a growl of fury. Latharn darted toward him with an enraged snarl of his own, ignoring Horas's cry of warning as he launched into a sword fight with the guard. Two other guards rushed out of the dungeons, engaging with his men while Latharn whirled, knocking out his attacker with the hilt of his sword.

While Horas and his other men continued to fight the guards, Latharn grabbed the keys off the fallen guard. Latharn, his brother and several other men then hurried into the dungeons. A dank and foul smell permeated the dungeons, which were lit only by a single torch. His body tightened with rage at the thought of Eibhlin being held in such a place.

He heard groans from one of the cells—male groans.

"Go tae them," he said, turning to his brother and his men. "I'll find Eibhlin."

His heart thudding with dread, he moved forward, searching each of the empty cells, until he reached an isolated one in the rear of the dungeons.

He froze at the sight of Eibhlin's form inside. She lay on her side, facing away from him, curled up into a protective ball like a bairn. Quelling his panic, he fumbled with the keys in his hand, trying several before successfully unlocking her cell door.

She stiffened at the sound of footsteps, and as he drew near, she shot to her feet, her leg flying toward his chest. He managed to evade her just in time, stepping back and holding up his hands to show her who he was.

Eibhlin went still as she took him in. Bruises marred her lovely face, and her golden eyes were haunted. Fury spread through his veins; Padraig would die a slow death at his hands.

"Latharn." Eibhlin's voice cracked, and she dissolved into sobs.

He moved toward her, enfolding her into the warmth of his arms as she wept.

"Ye're safe now, Eibhlin," he whispered. He swung her up into his arms and carried her out of the dungeons. She leaned into him, cradling her head against his chest.

A foreign, powerful emotion swept over him. Before now, his fight against Padraig was about family honor and his birthright. But now, it was about so much more. He would make the bastard suffer for what he had done to his Eibhlin—and he would ensure that she never came to harm again.

CHAPTER 16

*E*velyn was dimly aware of voices around her as she drifted in and out, torn between sleep and dreams, memory and nightmare.

After Padraig confronted her in the hall, his men had dragged her, kicking and screaming, down to the dungeons. There she'd waited, terrified, for what seemed like hours, until Padraig entered.

She backed up against the wall as he approached her with the calm lethality of a panther, his cold gray eyes trained on her face.

"I should have recognized those bastard's eyes," he hissed. "The man who wouldnae accept my father as chief and laird. Yer traitor of a father."

"Yer father was the traitor," she returned.

Padraig slapped her with such force she crumpled to the floor. Shock and fury whipped through her, greater than the pain of her throbbing cheek.

Padraig squatted down to her level, yanking her up by the hair. Recalling her self-defense training, she lifted her knee to kick him in the groin. Pleasure coiled through her as he stumbled back with a pained cry.

"Ye bitch!" Padraig snarled, again grabbing her by her hair and slamming her against the wall. "Ye're going tae tell me what I want tae ken about that bastard Latharn MacUisdean. And then I'm going tae enjoy this bonnie body of yers before I strangle the life from ye."

He spat in her face, releasing her so abruptly she sank to the ground. She didn't let the fear that his words invoked in her show. Instead, she gave him a look of defiance as she stumbled to her feet.

"Try," she snarled. She would kill the bastard before he could ever violate her in such a way.

Padraig glared down at her before his lips curved into a dangerous smile; a smile that caused a sliver of unease to coil around her belly.

He took out a dagger from its sheath on his belt and approached her.

"Where is Latharn MacUisdean?"

Don't show your fear, she told herself. *Never show your fear.*

"Dead," she replied, not allowing her eyes to stray from his.

He swore an oath, pinning both of her hands to the wall above her head with one hand and pressing his dagger to her throat with the other. Fear clawed at her chest, and her heart slammed violently against her ribcage, but she kept her gaze steady.

"Where is Latharn MacUisdean?" he repeated on a growl.

"Dead."

He asked her the question again and again, pressing the dagger to different parts of her body, but never hard enough to draw blood. She realized that this was his way of torture—the threat of him slicing her with the dagger was always there, and she didn't know when he would strike. Though her fear was so great she could choke on it, she betrayed none of it, repeating only that Latharn was dead—until she almost believed her own lie.

She didn't know how much time had passed when he finally stepped back with a frustrated snarl.

"When I return, I'll start carving up that bonnie face of yers. And then I'll have my men hold ye down and take their turns with ye until ye tell me what I want tae ken."

He left her alone, and only then did she allow herself to dissolve into tears, shaking with terror. She was certain she was going to die in this cell. She cursed herself for her foolishness in trusting Aimil, for not being more careful, for failing to avenge her father. But her heart ached most of all at the thought of never seeing Latharn again.

More time passed. Hours? Days? She heard pained screams and moans from the other prisoners, and dread gnawed away at her gut, knowing it would soon be her turn.

When Latharn entered her cell, she thought she was dreaming, that he couldn't be real.

Now, she awoke with a jerk, wondering with terror if her rescue had in fact been a dream, and she was still in that cell.

But she was in a large chamber, and Latharn sat at her bedside, his concerned gaze trained on her face. Relief flooded her with such force that tears sprang to her eyes.

"How are ye?" he asked gruffly. His eyes were shadowed; it looked like he hadn't slept. Her gaze slid outside—it was dark.

"I'm fine," she lied, blinking back her tears. "How long have I been out?"

"All day. 'Tis just after nightfall, but ye need rest," he said, reaching out to give her hand a gentle squeeze.

"I—I want ye tae ken. I didnae say anything tae Padraig," she said. "I insisted that ye were dead."

He dropped her hand, his mouth tightening as he glared at her.

"Is that what ye think I care about?" he rasped.

His anger took her by surprise. "I just thought—"

"All I could think of was getting tae ye, Eibhlin. I donnae care about myself. When I came intae that cell, and saw ye lying there, not moving—" His voice caught, and he closed his eyes, expelling a shuddering breath. "All that mattered tae me was that ye were all right. 'Tis all that matters. I'll make Padraig pay for what he's done," he swore, his gaze

146

lingering on her bruised face, anger flashing in his eyes before it was replaced by despair. "What happened is my fault, Eibhlin. I never should have allowed ye tae spy for me, tae return tae the castle—"

"No. It was my choice. I kent what the risks were."

"Well, I'll not let ye come tae harm again—I swear it," he said fiercely. "As soon as ye're rested, Horas will escort ye out of the Highlands and tae Inverness. There are docks there; ye can book passage back tae the Lowlands or anywhere ye wish tae go. I'll make certain ye have plenty of coin."

"Latharn, I donnae want tae—"

"No," he interrupted, his expression hardening. "This is what I should have done before. I'll not let harm come tae ye again. I'm sending ye away."

Pain sluiced through her at his words as he stood.

"I'll have Aoife bring ye food," he said. "Until then, ye must rest."

He left before she could issue another word of protest.

Maybe he's right, she thought, after Aoife brought her a meal moments later. She had done everything she could; she certainly couldn't return to the castle. Latharn had a growing number of men.

And now she had the memory of her time locked in that cell, terrified as she waited for rape, torture, death—or all three. She knew that her time imprisoned in that cell would continue to haunt her; those dark memories could lessen in her own time.

Yet her time here still felt unfinished, and she knew her resistance to leaving was because of Latharn. Her feelings for him ran deep, and even though she knew there could be nothing between her and the future laird of MacUisdean Castle, she wasn't ready to leave him behind.

If you insist on staying longer, she told herself, *you can't keep lying to him. You'll have to tell him the truth.*

A strange sense of calm settled over her as she came to this realization. She'd wanted to tell him the truth before but had feared his response. Now that he was determined to send her away, she had nothing to lose. *You'll lose Latharn,* a phantom voice whispered. But she didn't have him—and she never would.

When Aoife came to collect her finished meal, she asked which chamber Latharn was sleeping in. Aoife looked startled at her request but told her he was in the chamber at the end of the hall. Eibhlin nodded her thanks.

She waited until the din of voices from the distant corners of the manor receded into silence. Only then did she make her way to Latharn's chamber. The door was unlocked, and she took a deep breath before turning the knob and entering.

Her heart clenched as it always did at the sight

of his, tall, dark and handsome form, which was facing away from her as he gazed out the window.

He turned, looking startled at the sight of her.

"Eibhlin. What are ye doing here?"

She closed the door behind her and approached him, her mouth dry.

"I'm here tae tell ye I'm not going anywhere," she said, her voice wavering. "And," she continued, dropping her brogue and switching to her modern accent, "that I'm not where you think I'm from."

Latharn froze, his eyes going wide.

"You once asked me to tell you what I was hiding. Well . . . here it is. My name is both Eibhlin Aingealag O'Brolchan *and* Evelyn Angelica O'Brolchan," she whispered. It was difficult to speak with her mouth so dry, but she forced herself to continue. "The second is the modern, Anglicized form of my name. I was born in the fourteenth century, but I live in the twenty-first. I've . . . I've traveled through time to be here."

EVELYN WATCHED Latharn as she finished her story. She'd just told him everything, and watched as a range of emotions flickered across his face as her words settled in. Disbelief, anger, confusion and back to disbelief. She recalled feeling the same emotions when her mother first told her she was a time traveler.

When Latharn finally looked at her, she braced

herself for his anger. But there was still only a look of dazed disbelief on his face.

"Yer mother was a time traveler as well?"

"Yes," she said. "I didn't believe her when she told me at first."

It was odd to speak in her modern-day American accent after she'd spoken in the same brogue as everyone else in this time since she'd arrived. She could tell her natural accent discombobulated Latharn as well; his eyes narrowed as she spoke.

"And yer father kent?"

"Yes," she said. "He also didn't believe her at first . . . but he'd already fallen in love with her by then."

He turned away from her and began to pace, raking his hand through his hair.

"The laird I used tae work for—Artair Dalaigh— he recently wed. He also mentioned his bride, Diana, going tae Tairseach. She's a Sassenach, but her accent differs from other Sassenachs I've heard speak."

Evelyn stiffened. Her mother had never met another time traveler in the past, but she'd believed there were others.

"Do you think she's—" Evelyn began.

"I donnae ken," he said. "I—I've heard tales of strange happenings around Tairseach. My mother used tae tell me it was the faeries who stole people from Tairseach when I was a bairn."

"Not fairies," Evelyn said, with a wry smile. "Time." He didn't return her smile, and her heart sank. "Latharn, I understand if you don't believe me, but I—"

"Ye've been nothing but trustworthy, Eibhlin —*Evelyn*," he corrected himself. "I believe ye have no reason tae lie . . . especially after what ye've just been through."

Her heart lifted. He hadn't admitted to believing her, but at least he didn't think she was lying to him. It was a start.

"The time ye're from. The—future," he said, seeming to force the word past his lips. "It must be safe for ye there, aye?"

Evelyn stiffened, knowing where this was going.

"Yes," she hedged. "But Latharn, things are different in my time. Women are more independent; they can fight. I've trained in archery and sword fighting. I was scared when Padraig captured me, but I held my own against him. I can take care of myself. I want to stay not just to avenge my parents—I want to help you. After working among the servants, I know they're terrified of Padraig. They deserve a fair and kind laird—and I believe that laird is you."

Latharn's expression softened, but he still looked divided. "I cannae allow ye tae put yerself in harm's away again."

"I'm not going anywhere, Latharn."

Latharn glowered at her, but she returned his glare. He finally expelled a sigh and approached her, moving his hands up to cup the sides of her face.

"I kent there was something different about ye, lioness. From the moment I first laid eyes upon ye. But I never would have kent that ye're from another time."

"I know it sounds mad, but it's the truth. I've traveled through time to be here. Let me help you, Latharn."

He rested his forehead on hers, closing his eyes. When he opened them, they were a storm of conflict.

"If anything happens again—"

"It won't," she said fiercely. "And even if it does . . . you should know—Padraig likely has sore balls right now. I think he's afraid of me."

His eyes widened, and he let out a chuckle.

"My Evelyn," he murmured. "My lioness."

His eyes went smoky with desire; he captured her lips with his. She hungrily returned his kiss, wrapping her arms around him as he held her close.

"I have so many questions," he rasped, when he released her, "about yer time, and how ye got here. And ye need tae heal. But God, I want ye with a ferocity I can hardly bear, my Evelyn."

"I am healed," she whispered, as he began to pepper kisses along her jaw, causing sparks of electricity to dance along her skin. She didn't want to spend her time alone, with only the dark memories from her imprisonment as company. She wanted —*needed*—Latharn. "And I can answer any questions you have. Later," she said, her voice dropping with meaning.

Latharn let out a growl. He stood, and she gasped as he hefted her up into his arms, bridal style, carrying her toward the bed, a fierce hunger in his eyes.

CHAPTER 17

The wild tale Evelyn had just told him faded from Latharn's mind; all he could focus on now was his burning desire for her and his need to protect her. To claim her.

He plundered her lips with his as he lowered her to the bed. Evelyn wound her arms around his neck, moaning in a way that made his cock stir with arousal.

She reached up to disrobe him of his tunic and kilt, and he removed her underdress, his breath hitching in his throat at the sight of her perky breasts capped with rosy nipples, the flat expanse of her abdomen, the apex of her thighs and her glistening quim. Her body was a feast for the eyes; he allowed himself to take it in for a moment, until he could hold himself back no longer.

He let out a groan, lowering his head to her nipple, suckling on it as she arched toward him. She whimpered as he kneaded her breast before moving his mouth to her other nipple, suckling it thoroughly. Only then did he pepper kisses down along the long expanse of her abdomen. He knelt before her, spreading her legs wide. He looked up at her, meeting her eyes as he leaned forward to taste the sweetness between her thighs.

"Latharn . . ."

His name escaped from her lovely lips on a moan, and he luxuriated in the sound of her pleasure, the taste of her sweetness as he lapped at her. Her breath quickened, and she arched, her lovely breasts peaking upward.

"Ye're delicious, lass," he growled, grasping her thighs as he continued to taste her, and she shook and quivered beneath his tongue.

"Latharn!" she cried, as her release claimed her. He kept his gaze trained on her as she succumbed to the force of her release, her lovely body shaking, her eyes fluttering, her hands grasping the sheets. It was the most seductive sight he'd ever seen; he burned it into his memory.

Only when she'd caught her breath did he remove his mouth from her center, licking her skin up to her abdomen, her breasts, her throat, until he hovered above her.

She looked up at him, her face flushed, her breaths still rapid, arching her lovely body toward him.

"Latharn," she moaned. "Please . . ."

He obliged her with a groan, sinking inside her warmth as he kept his eyes locked on hers. She felt like heaven around him, and he had to clench his teeth to hold still, to allow her to get used to his length. After a few, torturous moments he began to move, slowly, afraid that he would instantly reach his release at the glorious feel of her.

Evelyn moaned, wrapping her legs around him and reaching down to grasp his buttocks. His lioness locked eyes with him, licking her dry lips.

"Don't hold back," she rasped. "Please . . ."

Her words, her beauty, and the feel of her undid him. He increased the pace of his thrusts, his breath coming out in guttural gasps as they moved together. Her body seemed made for him, and his for hers, as their nude bodies writhed together in that primal, eternal rhythm.

"Oh God . . . " Evelyn breathed, her eyes closing in bliss. He suckled at the base of her throat as he moved, reveling in the feel of her sweet tightness around his cock. Her hair was spread out behind her, like a curtain of fire; it was just as he'd imagined in his dreams.

"Ye're beautiful, Evelyn," he rasped.

He wanted to savor their lovemaking, but he knew he wouldn't be able to hold back his release for much longer; her tightness felt too perfect around his cock.

"Look at me, lioness," he whispered, and those striking eyes of hers opened, focusing on him. He leaned down to suckle at a rosy breast, and she shuddered, letting out a delirious cry as another release claimed her.

He watched her shudder with possessive pride before he increased the pace of his thrusts, and he groaned as his climax roiled through him. He spilled himself inside her, keeping his eyes locked on hers until his body stilled.

As they caught their breaths, he looped a leg around her and tugged her into the crook of his arm, burying his face in her hair.

Silence stretched between them for several moments; there was only the sign of their rapid breaths and the crackling of the fire in the fireplace. He adjusted himself to look down at her.

"Tell me," he said quietly, reaching out to wrap several strands of flame-red hair around his finger. "Tell me about yer time. And all about ye. From the beginning."

She froze, startled eyes meeting his.

"You believe me?"

"I donnae believe ye're a liar," he replied. "Nor do I believe ye're mad. Aye, I believe ye, Evelyn."

Ever since her confession, Evelyn seemed lighter, as if the confession had dislodged an invisible weight from her shoulders; the burden of her secret was no longer bearing down on her. He detected no lingering tension. He could only believe that she'd told him nothing but the truth—as mad as it seemed.

And there was the memory of Artair's bride, Diana, at their wedding; her cryptic words to him. *I think you'll find happiness of your own with a bonnie lass. And sooner than you think.*

Had Diana been referring to Evelyn? If so, how had she known? Was she a time traveler as well? When he saw Artair again, he had many questions for his former laird.

"I can tell that your mind is racing," she said. "I know you have questions."

"Aye," he said. "How can I not? But I doubt I'd be able tae understand it even if ye could explain how ye traveled through centuries."

"I couldn't explain that to you—I don't know how it works, only that I can do it," she said, giving him a wry smile. "Some days I still pinch myself when I wake up here. I can hardly believe all this myself."

"Tell me about ye," he repeated, aching for more knowledge about her. "Everything about ye in this future time."

She sat up, propping her head on her elbow.

"My mother raised me in a city called Seattle. It will be a city in lands not discovered yet. I thought my father had died of an illness when I was a baby . . . until Mom told me the truth. That's when I learned about Tairseach, stiuireadh, time travel . . . all of it."

He listened intently as she described this distant future dominated by something she called "technology": carriages without horses, buildings as tall as hills and mountains, vast lands on the other side of the ocean. She told him about her mother's life in this time, that she had a profession of her own—as many women did. Evelyn told him how she'd studied this time period at university, knowing that she would one day return to the time in which she was born.

"Ever since my mother told me her secret, I've always felt torn between two time periods—even though I'd never lived in the past," Evelyn mused.

"It seems like ye've only been focused on the past and the tragedy of what happened tae yer father, even when ye were in yer own time," he said. "Did ye not enjoy a life of yer own, separate from what yer mother told ye? Separate from the past?"

"How could I focus on anything else?" she said, her body tensing with defensiveness. "If you learned you'd been born centuries in the past, how would you react?"

"Ye forget that I did learn something life changing about my birth," he reminded her. "I'm glad my parents didnae tell me sooner, though I was at first angered. I was able tae live a normal life with my siblings, tae enjoy my time as a bairn and a youth. Had I kent what I ken now, I never would have had peace. All I'm suggesting tae ye, lass, is that when ye return," he continued, his heart clenching at the thought, "ye focus on yer life in that time—and yer life alone."

"It'll be hard for me, Latharn. Ever since my mother died, I feel like this time has connected me to her. Letting go of this time period will feel like letting go of her . . . and my father's memory. But I know she'd want me to move forward with my life.

So . . . I'll try," Evelyn said, after a brief pause and a strained smile.

He suppressed the pain that spread through his chest at the thought of her eventual departure. But she would be safe in this future she spoke of. As for Latharn, he had to wed a noble lass to secure his claim.

Even as he told himself this, there was something that still bothered him, though it should have been none of his concern. He had no permanent claim on her.

"Ye're not a virgin," he said, before he could stop himself.

Evelyn leaned back, arching an eyebrow.

"Neither are you," she coolly returned.

"'Tis different for me," he protested. "Ye're—"

"In my time," Evelyn **i**nterrupted, giving him a firm look, "many women my age aren't virgins. It's not common for women to wait for marriage until they bed a man. So yes, I've had a lover," she said.

A wave of jealousy swept over him, and he clenched his jaw.

"But," she continued, her tone softening as she reached out to touch the side of his face, "no one has ever made love to me like that. I might as well have been a virgin."

Her face flamed, and male pride overtook his jealousy. He grinned down at her, though he still longed to put her other lover to his blade. It was best that this man was in another time, far from his reach.

"Are you jealous, Latharn MacUisdean?" Evelyn teased, studying his fierce expression with a grin.

"Aye," he admitted. There was no use denying it. "I donnae like the thought of any other man enjoying yer lovely body."

A look of delight flared in her eyes before it was gone again.

"I'm the one who should be jealous," she said. "I'm not the one who will soon wed someone else."

"It willnae be soon," he said, but her expression darkened; his words didn't seem to reassure her. "I —I donnae want tae wed, but I must. It may not be for some time, and it will only be for purposes of—"

"You don't have to explain yourself," Evelyn interrupted. "I know you have your duties. And after I help you take down that bastard, I'll be able to return to my time with a lighter heart, knowing I've avenged my father in my own way."

But her smile didn't reach her eyes, and his stomach again clenched at the thought of Evelyn disappearing into the fabric of time.

"We must savor the time we do have together," he said, winding his hand in her hair and tugging her close. "But I'll not have ye putting yerself in danger again. Ye must do everything I say if ye're tae remain."

A flash of that familiar defiance shone in her eyes before it dissipated, and she expelled a sigh.

"All right," she muttered.

To his surprise, she moved out of his arms,

exposing every inch of her beautiful body to his hungry eyes as she climbed out of bed. She reached for her underdress, and he scowled.

"Where are ye going?" he demanded.

"It's best if I don't sleep in your bed," she said, not looking at him as she slipped on her underdress. "The others will know."

Latharn climbed out of bed, yanking her to him with a growl.

"Aoife is discreet, and my men have no reason tae come tae my chamber," he said. "Ye'll stay in my bed while we're lovers. And," he added, nipping at her ear as another surge of desire flowed through him, "I've not finished with ye, lioness. I intend," he continued, maneuvering her back to the bed and lowering her gown, settling himself between her thighs, "tae make use of every moment I have with ye, starting now."

CHAPTER 18

*T*he next morning, Evelyn tried to keep her expression neutral as she stood next to Latharn. They were gathered before a dozen of his men in the large drawing room.

The night before had been . . . glorious. There was no other word to describe it. After they'd made love a second time, they'd fallen asleep entwined in each other's arms.

Earlier that morning, they'd simply held each other, listening to the sound of the Highlands in the morning; the distant sound of horse hooves, birds cawing, the whisper of the dawn breeze.

It was in the quiet of the dawn that Evelyn had proposed to Latharn how she could help going forward, and to her relief, Latharn had agreed. But he'd wanted to share with his men her continued involvement—most would assume she would be on her way after her ordeal of being captured.

Now, nervousness spiraled through her as she

met each man's gaze, which ranged from mildly curious to borderline hostile. It was one thing to work as a spy in the castle and another thing altogether to work alongside a group of the burly Highlanders who now followed Latharn.

"As ye may ken, Eibhlin's father was Tormod Ualan O'Brolchan," Latharn said. "He was killed by my uncle for his loyalty tae my father. To avenge him, and for his honor, 'tis her desire tae keep working alongside us until I've removed Padraig from power and take my rightful place."

"She nearly got herself killed by Padraig," Gormal said with a scowl. "What can the lass help with? I hope ye're not suggesting she fight."

He started to reply, but it was Evelyn who spoke up.

"No," she said, setting her nervousness aside as she stepped forward. "Though I'm probably a better archer than many of yer men. But there is something I can do tae help that none of ye can."

It was odd to speak in her affected accent now that Latharn knew who she truly was, but it was vital she keep up the ruse with the others. It was best that the rest of these men didn't know she was a twenty-first century time traveler; she suspected they wouldn't be as understanding as Latharn.

"And what is that?" Horas asked. Unlike Gormal, he wasn't glaring at her; he looked genuinely curious.

"I can talk tae the women of Clan Creagach," she said. "My mother was friendly with some of the noble wives; I'm hoping they remember her. The wives of nobles are more influential then ye all ken —or as some of ye may already ken," she added, giving the men a knowing look.

Several of the men looked amused and even chuckled at her words.

"I may not be wed, but I think ye speak truth, lass," Horas said, his eyes twinkling.

"Aye," Baigh added, his own eyes alight with amusement. "As someone wed tae quite the wife, Eibhlin speaks truth."

"I can talk tae them, persuade them tae convince their husbands tae join Latharn if they're still hesitant," she said. This was what she'd proposed to Latharn this morning; by the looks in the men's eyes before her, she could see that at least some of them were amenable to the idea.

"Now," Latharn said, "we need tae prepare for what's next."

Everyone dispersed: some men off to training drills to prepare for the eventual battle, while Latharn had a private meeting with Gormal to discuss his upcoming meeting with the chief of Clan Creagach.

"I want Horas and Tulach tae train ye tae defend yerself," Latharn told her, as everyone dispersed. "I donnae want what happened with Padraig tae happen again."

She almost refused, wanting to remind him that she'd already had such training in her own time, but Latharn gave her a firm look. And, she grudgingly reminded herself, her training hadn't prevented her from being captured.

"Please, Evelyn," he murmured, his words low enough for only her to hear as he spoke her true name, and a shiver snaked down her spine. Her eyes dropped to his lips, recalling how those lips had felt on her body last night.

She obediently turned to trail after Horas and Tulach to stop herself from salivating over Latharn with other people present.

Nothing has changed. He has his duty, she reminded herself. *And you have your duty as well. You have to focus.*

HORAS AND TULACH were thoroughly impressed with Evelyn during her brief training session with them. She easily outperformed them during archery practice, and held her own when Horas taught her how to fight using a dagger.

"Where did ye learn such skills, lass?" Horas asked, his eyes wide with amazement.

"An uncle liked tae teach me how tae defend myself," she lied.

"I'd like tae meet this uncle of yers," Tulach grunted, rubbing his arm where she'd struck him during a practice fight, and she laughed.

After her training with Horas and Tulach, she didn't see Latharn for the rest of the day. She finally saw him at supper, looking achingly handsome as always: his dark hair sexily disheveled, his whiskey-colored eyes filled with concentration as he spoke to Gormal. She knew he was insecure about his past as a servant, but seated at the head of the table, surrounded by his men, he looked every inch a leader. She tried hard to not stare at him, but that was like trying to avoid the pull of a magnet.

"He'll make a fine leader," Tulach said, catching one of her stray gazes at Latharn.

Tulach was seated at her side, and she flushed, hoping he didn't guess the true reason for her stares, but he looked lost in his own thoughts.

"His uncle Steaphan MacUisdean let my family starve when he was laird," Tulach continued, his eyes shadowing with grief. "It was a harsh winter, and they didnae have enough coin for rent. He took much of their stores of food for payment. My parents ate little, so we could eat. My father didnae survive the winter."

Anger and sympathy roiled through her, and she clenched her fists at her side. She'd suspected there was some deeper reason that had propelled Tulach to work for Latharn.

"I'm sorry, Tulach," she murmured.

"Padraig is just like his father; he doesnae care for the common folk. But Latharn—he hasnae kent wealth. He kens what 'tis like tae struggle. And he's a good man. I ken no other family will suffer like mine did when he's laird."

She nodded her agreement, pride swelling in her chest. Latharn would give up his own food stores rather than let anyone else starve. There was kindness and empathy in every pore of his handsome body.

The men around her abruptly fell silent, and she turned as Latharn got to his feet.

"I wanted ye all tae ken that the chieftain of Clan Creagach has agreed tae meet with me tomorrow. We'll discuss an alliance then," he said. His gaze shifted to hers, and Evelyn couldn't help but bask in his gaze, which was like the warming rays of the sun. "Eibhlin will accompany me tae meet with his wife and the other noble wives tae persuade their men tae join our cause."

All eyes turned to her. She swallowed hard and gave him a nod. After hearing Tulach's story, she was more determined than ever to succeed.

Latharn didn't come to her bed that night, and she tossed and turned, desire for him humming throughout her body when she finally fell into a restless sleep, which was punctuated by nightmares of her time in the cell with Padraig.

When she awoke, she forced aside the memory of her nightmares, her need for Latharn still coursing through her. She had to concentrate as she washed and dressed in a borrowed gown that Aoife had picked up from a wife of one of Latharn's allies.

She entered the dining room to find a dozen

men already gathered as Aoife placed platters of food down. She tried to keep her hunger for Latharn out of her eyes as he stood and approached her. Even at barely past dawn he looked gorgeous, wearing a dark tunic and belted plaid kilt with not a strand of dark hair out of place. At the sight of him, her heart did a brief catapult in her chest.

"Good morning tae ye," he said. "Are ye ready tae speak tae Lady Reuda Creagach?"

His voice was loud enough for the others to hear and oddly impersonal; she realized that he wanted the appearance of talking "business" with her while the others were within earshot.

"Aye," she said.

This was only a half truth. She'd mostly fantasized about Latharn and had to force herself to remain in her chamber and not seek him out the night before.

"Good," he said. "What do ye think ye'll discuss?"

He held out his hand, gesturing for her to follow, and as soon as they were out of the room, he took her hand, leading her into an empty adjoining chamber, pressing her against the wall. Her eyes widened in surprise as he seized her mouth with his in a passionate kiss. She whimpered against his mouth as his tongue probed hers, his arms wrapping around her waist to press her flush against his hard, muscular body.

"I ached for ye last night, but Gormal came tae my chamber tae review what I was tae say today," he murmured, when he finally released her. "I'd much rather have enjoyed yer company last night, lioness."

Joy flooded her at his words; he shifted so that she could feel his arousal, and a torrent of desire swept over her. He kissed her once more, and she returned it, clinging to him like he was a life raft amid a tumultuous ocean, until they were forced to break apart for air. Latharn rested his forehead against hers, his voice low and husky as he spoke.

"It will be difficult tae keep my hands and eyes off ye today," he murmured. He expelled a sigh, stepping back from her: regret, and something she couldn't identify flickering in his eyes. "But I must."

As if to accentuate his point, the deep rumble of his men's voices filled the corridor as they left the dining room. He lifted her hand to his in a brief kiss before leaving her behind with a growing ache of longing between her thighs—and in her heart.

CHAPTER 19

*L*atharn stood across from Chieftain Modan Creagach, who studied him with an unreadable expression. Modan was a broad bull of a man, with red hair that had gone silver at the temples, and black eyes that reminded Latharn of a hawk's.

They were gathered in the great hall of Clan Creagach's seat, Creagach Castle. Latharn and his men stood before Modan and his nobles, who all flanked him at the long head table. Latharn had just proposed that they work together as allies against Padraig.

Modan had not responded, and now a long silence stretched. Latharn suspected the silence was supposed to intimidate him, but he steadily held Modan's gaze.

"I donnae hold no great loyalty tae Padraig MacUisdean," Modan finally said. "I'd hoped his brother Neacal would become laird and chieftain instead; he has honor, unlike his brother."

Latharn tried not to bristle at the compliment toward Neacal, though Evelyn's words did enter his mind. *Padraig may be like his father, but I donnae think Neacal is.* But he pushed aside the thought.

"I wouldnae be here if I believed that Padraig was the best chieftain for Clan MacUisdean. I've spoken tae the common folk—and some nobles—about him. He's filled with greed and cruelty. If ye join with me tae—" Latharn began.

"We've had an alliance with Clan MacUisdean since before yer father was chief," Modan interrupted. "They have more men than we do. If they kent we've allied with ye, they'll attack."

"Yer men wouldnae have tae fight him alone," Latharn insisted. "Ye'll have the men who swore fealty tae me, and the men of the laird I once served, Artair Dalaigh."

Artair had offered his help before Latharn had returned here, but he'd resisted reaching out to him, wanting to take back his titles without the help of his former laird. It was Gormal who'd convinced him to reach out to Artair; they needed as many men on their side as possible to fight his cousin. Latharn had forced his pride aside, allowing Gormal to send a letter requesting Artair's assistance. Gormal had sent the letter the day before; Artair was a man of his word, and Latharn knew that he'd come with men when Latharn sent for him.

At his words, Modan fell silent again, turning to a dark-haired man at his side. The man murmured something Latharn couldn't hear before Modan turned back to face him.

"I'll need some time tae discuss yer proposal with my nobles."

Latharn tensed; he didn't want to leave until he had a clear answer. If he left now, he feared Modan would refuse to join him.

He opened his mouth to protest, but at his side, Gormal gave a subtle shake of his head.

"I will take my leave," Latharn said, after a brief pause. "It would be an honor tae join with ye in an alliance. Consider what I've said."

As they made their way out of the great hall, Gormal hurried to Latharn's side.

"Needing tae discuss with his nobles doesnae mean he'll refuse ye," Gormal said, but Latharn only offered him a grunt in response. If he couldn't get Clan Creagach to ally with him—and they joined with Padraig instead—it would make defeating his cousin even more difficult.

When they returned to the manor, he found Evelyn with Tulach and the others. By the brow-beaten expression on her face, it looked as if her meeting with Lady Creagach hadn't gone well.

He gathered his men in the drawing room, where he told them how the meeting with Modan had gone, trying to not show how defeated he felt.

"Brother," Crisdean spoke up, when Latharn fell silent. Crisdean's gaze slid briefly to Evelyn before he continued. "I think Eibhlin's earlier suggestion of reaching out tae Neacal was a fine one. Even Modan mentioned that he had honor. Perhaps Neacal can—"

"No," Latharn interrupted, giving his brother a scowl.

"My laird," Baigh hedged. "I agree with yer brother. If we can get Neacal tae work with us, perhaps we'd have no need for Clan Creagach."

Several other men muttered their agreement. He met Evelyn's eyes; she gave him a hopeful look. He tore his gaze away.

"Going tae Neacal would be a great risk," he said. "If we're wrong about him, he'll hang me and the rest of ye as well. We still have Artair Dalaigh's men who'll fight alongside us—and I'm not giving up on Clan Creagach."

"My laird," Gormal said, stepping forward. "I agree that going tae Neacal is a risk. Ye need tae focus on the best way tae secure an alliance—and that's marriage. Padraig is focused on finding a bride from a clan larger than Clan Creagach. As such, Chieftain Creagach has two daughters, both unwed. If ye offer tae wed his eldest daughter, that would be an attractive prospect."

Latharn's chest tightened. He shouldn't have been surprised; Gormal had already suggested that he wed a lass from Clan Creagach. It took everything in his power to not look at Evelyn.

"He's right."

He stilled; it was Evelyn who'd spoken up. He turned to look at her. She held her head high, and though she'd gone slightly pale, she met his gaze.

"Offering tae wed his daughter will help ye secure an alliance with his clan," she continued.

Gormal looked both pleased and surprised at her agreement, while Latharn noticed that Crisdean looked troubled, but said nothing.

He swallowed, ignoring the twisting pain in his heart. He'd known this day was coming, that he would have to wed to solidify his claim. But he felt nothing but dread, like he was a prisoner being led to the dungeons for execution.

"Very well," he said. "Send a messenger and inform the chieftain that I will wed his eldest daughter—if he allies with me."

Evelyn disappeared after the meeting; she didn't even come down for supper. He almost went to her chamber that night but made himself stay away; he didn't know how she'd receive him now that he had a pending marriage proposal out to another lass.

Though he already missed her, he was relieved that he didn't see her the next morning as well—he needed to look convincing when presented with wedding Modan's daughter. Evelyn's presence would make that difficult.

When they entered the great hall of Creagach Castle, Modan and his nobles were far more welcoming than they'd been the day before. Modan even stood to greet them, a wide smile spreading across his face.

"I've discussed yer proposal with my nobles and my wife," Modan said. "I accept—and I accept yer offer of an alliance. Ye will wed my eldest daughter, Ros."

"I am honored, Chieftain Creagach," he said, with a forced smile, ignoring the hollowness that spread throughout his gut. "I'm hoping we can discuss a strategy tae—"

"Later," Modan interrupted. "I'd like for ye tae meet Ros, and then we can discuss details of the battle tae come."

Dread twisted Latharn's heart, but he gave him a jerky nod.

"I'd be honored, Chieftain Creagach."

"She's waiting for ye in one of the back gardens," Modan said, gesturing to a servant who hurried forward to escort Latharn out of the hall.

The servant led Latharn to a private garden in the rear of the castle grounds, where a young woman stood next to her mother Reuda, a severe-looking woman with green eyes and dark hair, and two maids. They all bowed before leaving him alone with Ros.

Ros was bonnie, with her mother's dark hair and her father's sharp, dark eyes. But he felt nothing: no trace of desire. A glimpse of Evelyn filled his mind; her silken hair wrapped around his fingers, his lips on her skin. He forced away the images as he stepped forward.

"'Tis an honor tae meet ye," he said.

Ros opened her mouth to speak, but no words came. Instead, she burst into tears.

Startled, he led her to a stone bench where she pressed her hands to her face as her shoulders shook with silent sobs.

"I—I'm sorry, my laird," she whispered, when her tears subsided. "It—it willnae happen again. 'Tis my honor tae meet ye as well."

"What is the reason for yer tears?"

"'Tis not important," she said quickly. "Please donnae tell my parents that I wept."

"Lass," he said gently, "ye can tell me. I'll not be angered."

Ros expelled a sigh, searching his face as if looking for reassurance. He remained silent but gave her an encouraging nod.

"I—there's someone else I care for. Someone my father will never allow me tae wed," she whispered. "But I still have my maidenhead, my laird. I swear it."

A torrent of relief washed over him.

"Do ye wish tae marry this man?" he asked. "Ye can tell me the truth."

"Aye," she whispered, her eyes again filling with tears. "But I'll wed ye, as 'tis my duty—"

"There's no need tae make such promises," he said. "There's someone I care for as well. I have a proposal for ye—a proposal that will suit the both of us."

CHAPTER 20

*E*velyn remained in her chamber after Latharn left to seal his betrothal with Chieftain Creagach's daughter, grief tearing at her heart. As soon as she was alone, she sank to her knees, her body shaking with silent sobs.

It had taken everything in her power yesterday to agree with Gormal that Latharn needed to wed the chieftain's daughter, though her heart was tearing apart as she'd said the words. She'd gone out of her way to avoid him after that, pain and jealousy gnawing at her insides.

It was ironic that the same day Latharn sealed his engagement to another woman was the same day she realized she was in love with him. Desperately, painfully, deeply in love.

Her feelings had started with desire—he was insanely sexy, and the most handsome man she'd ever seen. But there was also an innate *goodness* to him. Claiming his titles was more than about obtaining wealth; he genuinely wanted to help the common folk of his father's clan. And that made her love him even more.

She knew the wise thing to do was to leave. Latharn had plenty of support around him, especially now that he was securing the alliance with Clan Creagach. She was the one who didn't belong here; this was Latharn's destiny all along, to wed a noblewoman, to become laird and chief. She couldn't watch him wed someone else. She didn't even think she could be around him when he was officially engaged.

But she still ached to remain near him for as long as possible. She was a fool; a lovesick fool. And like a fool, she'd spend as much time as she could here and return to her own time with a broken heart.

She thought about what Latharn had suggested, that she move on from the past and live her own life in the future. Her life in the future was empty; she'd been close to her mother, and after her death she'd felt . . . adrift. She'd sold the home they'd lived in and took odd teaching jobs to support her preparations to return to the past, not making any meaningful relationships.

Evelyn had spent so much of her time in the future preoccupied with the past and returning here that she hadn't truly considered what she'd do with the rest of her life once her task here was complete. She had briefly considered teaching in a university setting; after all, no one in the present was as aware of what life was like in the four-teenth century as she was. But she bristled at the thought of being stuck in a classroom or a lecture hall.

Perhaps she could teach medieval combat training at a fencing school. That sounded appealing, but an even more appealing thought occurred to her: teaching women of this time how to defend themselves. She allowed herself to briefly fantasize about what her life could be like in this time as Latharn's bride and his lady, using her status to teach lower-born women self-defense moves. She could even imagine Latharn giving her an approving nod as he watched her from the sidelines as she taught women how to use daggers, how he'd ignore the disapproval of the nobles at her very unladylike prowess.

But she forced the appealing thoughts to scatter, like ashes in the wind. Latharn needed to wed someone appropriate—and he didn't love her.

She resolved to keep her distance from Latharn, at least until her tumultuous feelings calmed, and she could look at him without wanting to burst into tears. She needed to find other ways to make herself useful now that her meeting with Lady Reuda Creagach hadn't gone well. It had been downright disastrous.

She'd thought Reuda would at least be polite to her, but as soon as a servant ushered her into the drawing room where Reuda was waiting, the older woman had glared at her.

"Are ye Latharn MacUisdean's whore?" Reuda had asked bluntly.

Evelyn looked at her in disbelief, struggling to tap down her anger.

"I'm—"

"Ye're the only lass in his company, and ye're quite bonnie," Reuda continued, spitting out the compliment. "Why are ye with him?"

"Because I'm his ally. His uncle killed my father—who ye kent," Evelyn said, trying to maintain a façade of calm, though rage was simmering inside her. "I want tae help Latharn because 'tis what my father would have wanted. I came tae see ye tae implore—"

But Reuda wouldn't let her finish, holding up her hand to silence her.

"Yer father was a good man, aye, but he is long dead. Ye're now a servant, and I've nothing tae discuss with a servant."

"Lady Creagach, with respect, I am no longer working as a servant. I am here as Latharn MacUisdean's guest and ally. I implore ye tae—"

"Donnae make me fetch my guard tae escort ye out," Reuda interrupted, her eyes flashing with hostility.

Evelyn left with her tail between her legs, when she'd wanted nothing more than to tell the snobby Lady Creagach off. But she had to remind herself that in this time class was everything; Reuda had every right to dismiss her. And if Reuda refused to hear her out, the other noble wives of the clan would likely do the same.

The sound of horse hooves pulled her from her maelstrom of thoughts, and she hurried to the window to see Latharn approach with Horas and Gormal. Her heart clenched at the sight of him, handsome as always, his dark hair windswept, his muscular arms rippling as he dismounted from his horse. A physical ache tore through her, and she stepped back from the window, blinking back tears. Had he sealed his betrothal to his bride-to-be with a kiss? Was his betrothed beautiful? Was he happy that he was going to wed?

She swallowed, turning to head out of her chamber. She needed to get out of the manor—perhaps to find Tulach for more self-defense training, or to take a walk—anything to avoid Latharn and take her mind off her heartbreak and jealousy.

But as she emerged from her chamber, she halted in her tracks. Latharn was striding toward her with purpose.

She almost fled back into her room, but Latharn seemed to guess her intention and quickened his strides, taking her by the arm.

"I need tae talk tae ye," he said, leading her back into her chamber.

She opened her mouth to refuse him, but they were already alone, and he was closing the door behind him.

"Latharn, you're betrothed," she said, trying to keep her voice from wavering. "You need to—"

185

"No," he said, "I'm not. At least not in truth."

Hope swelled in her chest.

"What—what do you mean?"

"The lassie is in love with someone else. I told her she can keep her lover, as long as she goes along with the pretense that we are tae be wed. Once the alliance is secure and I have my titles, we plan tae tell her father the truth."

A burst of joy exploded in her heart at the words, before unease settled in.

"But—if you go back on your word to wed the chieftain's daughter—"

"I can tell that Modan just wants his daughter to wed a noble from Clan MacUisdean, to further bind the alliance. I plan tae offer him a marriage between his other daughter and another noble of Clan MacUisdean," Latharn said.

Evelyn bit her lip, conflicted. She should tell Latharn that it was too risky to deceive the chieftain in this way, but her love for him made her selfish; she didn't want him betrothed to Modan's daughter—or to anyone.

"Ye were avoiding me," Latharn continued with a frown, reaching out to cup the side of her face. "Were ye jealous, Evelyn?"

"I was the one who agreed with Gormal," she said, licking her dry lips. She didn't want him to know she loved him; it would only complicate things further. "I knew it was best if you—"

"It wouldnae have caused ye grief if I'd kissed my betrothed? If we'd made love?" he asked, his voice dropping to a husky whisper as he stepped closer.

The jealousy that seized her was so potent she could taste it.

"It would have caused me great grief," she confessed. "So, yes. I would have been jealous."

To her irritation, he looked pleased. He leaned in to seize her lips, and her love and desire for him was too great to resist. His lips were firm and demanding against her own; he kissed her until she was breathless. He released her and stepped back, pinning her arms to her sides.

"What—what are ye—" she began, her voice dropping to a rasp as he hiked up her gown.

"I have tae return tae my men," he whispered, nipping at her lower lip. She gasped as his finger dipped into her center. "I donnae have time tae make love tae ye as I wish, tae show ye that ye are the only lass I desire. But that doesnae mean I cannae make ye come for me."

"Latharn . . . " she moaned, but his lips captured her moan as his finger began to stroke her in a tantalizing rhythm, in and out, in and out, as he plundered her mouth with his.

Evelyn reached up to clutch his broad shoulders, whimpering against his mouth, her pleasure building until it reached a crescendo, and her entire body quaked as her orgasm claimed her.

"Aye," he murmured, tearing his mouth away from hers as she threw her head back to let out a strangled cry. "Come for me, my beauty. My lioness."

The room seemed to shake around her, her body quivering her release, and when she stilled, Latharn rested his forehead on hers, his intense dark eyes focused on her face.

"While ye're here in this time," he whispered. "Ye're the only woman for me. Ye're mine. As I'm yers."

CHAPTER 21

"Clan Creagach welcomes ye, Latharn MacUisdean, true chieftain of Clan MacUisdean. We are happy tae ally with ye," Modan said, beaming at Latharn. "Now that ye are tae wed my daughter, ye'll be a son tae me. Family. And I'll fight for ye as my family."

The nobles who flanked Modan let out shouts of agreement; Latharn had to suppress his guilt. He met the eyes of Ros, who stood next to her father in the great hall where they'd gathered to officially announce their betrothal and alliance to the clan nobles. She paled slightly but kept a forced smile on her face. He knew she was nervous about their subterfuge, but it was necessary for the time being.

"My nobles have been sworn tae secrecy. There are some who still need convincing tae join yer side, but I'll make certain they do," Modan continued. "Padraig willnae ken that we are allies; he'll believe that we're still on his side. But from this day forward, our allegiance will lie with ye, Laird MacUisdean. Tonight, we celebrate with a feast. Ye and yer top men are welcome tae stay here in the castle; we already have guest chambers set aside."

"I thank ye for yer generosity, Chieftain Creagach," Latharn said. "I look forward tae our alliance."

And for appearance's sake, he stepped forward to take Ros's hands, raising them to his lips. He met her eyes, communicating his gratitude for her assistance with this farce, and she gave him a subtle nod of her head.

Modan looked pleased by his gesture, grinning as Latharn and his men were escorted from the great hall by a servant.

"Ye did well," Gormal said, giving him a look of pride as they trailed the servant to their guest chambers.

Latharn said nothing, merely nodding his head. No one besides Evelyn, Ros and his brother knew of his true plans, and he intended to keep it that way for as long as possible.

He spent the rest of his day meeting with Modan's nobles and his own men. He didn't see Evelyn until that night's feast, which was grand, the tables of the great hall heaped with succulent meats, wine and ale.

Latharn was seated at the head table next to Ros, but his eyes kept straying to Evelyn, who sat at the opposite end of the hall in between his brother and Tulach, not meeting his eyes.

"Is that yer lass?" Ros whispered in his ear, and he stiffened. He'd tried not to be obvious with his stares. "I can see why ye're taken with her," she continued at his nod, her eyes straying to Evelyn. "She's quite bonnie."

Evelyn looked even lovelier tonight in a gown of sapphire blue, her flame-red hair flowing loose around her shoulders. Her eyes met his for a brief second, darkening as they slid to Ros, before she turned away to focus on his brother.

"She looks like she wants tae pierce me with an arrow," Ros murmured with a chuckle.

Latharn smiled. He knew that his lioness's jealousy shouldn't please him, but it did. He liked that she was as possessive of him as he was of her.

"And the man ye love?" he asked in a low voice. Ros hadn't told him the name of her paramour, only that he was lowborn. "Is he here?"

"No," she whispered, pain flickering across her face. "He didnae want tae see me with ye, even though I told him it was only for appearances."

"This will be over soon," he murmured, giving her a look of sympathy. "And ye have my word; I'll try tae persuade yer father tae let ye marry the man ye love."

"Ye're not like other nobles," Ros said after a moment, studying him closely. "Any other man would have told my father my secret and then imprisoned me in their manor."

"Ye forget I'm not yet a laird. I spent my whole

life as—" He nodded toward a servant who was taking cups and refilling them.

"I cannae imagine not kenning who ye truly are. Tell me about yer time as a servant," she said, looking genuinely intrigued.

He did so, trying not to cast glances across the hall at Evelyn as he did so. Whenever he did manage to catch her eyes, she looked at him with a coldness that made his heart ache, and his amusement over her jealousy faded. Had she already forgotten his words to her—that she was the only woman for him? Didn't she understand that he was only doing this for appearances' sake? He and Ros needed to look content with their betrothal to make Modan happy. He wanted nothing more than to sit at Evelyn's side, to listen to her musical laughter, to take in the loveliness of her countenance.

The musicians began to play, and Modan turned to look at him and Ros with an expectant smile. He reluctantly got to his feet, taking Ros' hand and moving to the center of the hall.

Though Ros was a fine dancer, he felt nothing as they moved together, and he had to force a smile as they danced. She seemed just as uncomfortable, and when the musicians switched to a different song, she leaned in close.

"We're expected tae switch partners. Go dance with yer lady love."

He gave her a grateful smile and stepped back as Ros began to dance with another clan noble. He looked around, scowling when he saw that Evelyn was dancing with his brother. Gritting his teeth, he approached and glowered at Crisdean. Crisdean stepped away from Evelyn, giving Latharn a mischievous wink and a deep bow.

When he took Evelyn into his arms, she stood stiffly, and for a moment he feared she'd refuse him, before she finally relaxed. The feel of her in his arms was night and day from holding Ros; a firestorm of heat flared to life within his belly, and his cock stirred. If Evelyn noticed his arousal, she gave no indication, looking anywhere else but at him as they danced.

"Are you enjoying your time with your betrothed?" she asked stiffly.

"'Tis for appearances only," he murmured. "Ye ken this, Evelyn."

"It looked like you were enjoying keeping up appearances," she returned, raising her golden eyes to clash with his.

"I'll have ye ken," he said, pulling her even closer, "that we were discussing ye and how bonnie ye are."

Evelyn looked at him with openmouthed surprise. Grinning, he leaned in close, his lips fanning against her ear.

"Ros is a kind and bonnie lass—yet she leaves me cold. But ye, lioness," he whispered, "set every part of me aflame. I've barely been able tae keep my eyes off ye. Yer jealousy is unwarranted. 'Tis I who should be furious—ye were dancing quite close tae my brother. Do ye want me tae murder my own brother?"

"It would be fitting," she returned, but her mouth twitched in a smile. "I want to murder your betrothed."

"Instead of murdering anyone," he murmured, his eyes dancing with amusement, "come tae my bed tonight after the castle is sleeping."

The song ended, and he forced himself to step back from her, giving her a respectful nod. He made his way to Ros, escorting her back to their table, his senses still humming with desire for Evelyn.

When the feast came to an end, he escorted Ros from the hall, while Evelyn shot daggers at them with her eyes.

"Ye should spend time with yer beloved tonight," Ros said, once they left the hall. "I think she needs assurances as tae yer affections. And," she added, lowering her voice, "there are no guards posted on yer side of the castle late at night."

Latharn looked at her in surprise. Giving him a knowing smile, Ros disappeared down the corridor to her chamber. Ros Creagach wasn't as innocent as she appeared. He wondered if she had clandestine meetings with her lover under the cover of night.

He waited until the castle was utterly silent before slipping from his chamber to go to Evelyn's.

She was awake, standing by the window. She whirled as he entered, distress marring her lovely features.

"I know my jealousy is unreasonable—and self-ish," she said, as he approached. "Your betrothal shouldn't be for show—it should be in truth, Latharn. You need this alliance. I'm the one who doesn't belong, who isn't even from this time."

"I donnae care what time ye're from—I'm glad ye're here now, with me. I told ye before, I intend tae savor every moment I have with ye."

"But Latharn—"

"I donnae want tae hear anymore," he interrupted. "Ye were the loveliest lass in the hall tonight. I need ye, Evelyn."

He lifted her in his arms, carrying her over to the bed. He started to remove her underdress, but she stopped him. He froze; was she refusing him? But there was only hunger in her eyes.

"Let me," she whispered.

His mouth went dry as she removed her underdress, revealing her delectable body to his needy gaze. She reached out and disrobed him, removing his kilt and tunic before reaching out to clasp his buttocks, her golden eyes rising to meet his as she wrapped her lips around his cock.

"Evelyn . . ." he groaned, as she took him into her mouth, stroking him with her tongue.

A powerful ache rose within him; he knew he wouldn't last long, but he couldn't bring himself to stop her, throwing his head back as she moaned around him. The sound of her moan undid him, and he shuddered, spilling his release into her mouth.

He stumbled back, his chest heaving, as Evelyn looked up at him with a mischievous smile. Just the image of her, nude and on her knees before him, made his cock stir once more.

"My lioness," he growled, reaching down to pull her onto the bed. He seized one of her breasts, laving the rosy nipple with his tongue before settling over her, keeping his eyes locked with hers as he buried himself inside her.

"Latharn," she cried out, wrapping her legs around him as he rode her. He suckled at the base of her throat, her jaw, her lips.

"Look at me, Evelyn," he ordered, and she obliged, meeting his eyes as he gripped her buttocks, continuing to thrust inside her. "Ye are the only lass I see, lioness. The only one I crave. Ye've seared yerself into me, branded me as yer own. I never have—nor will I ever—long for a lass as I long for ye."

Emotion flared in her eyes, her golden eyes glistening as she gripped his shoulders.

"And I you," she whispered. "Latharn . . . Latharn, I—" she faltered, closing her eyes as a shudder of pleasure claimed her.

"What?" he asked, slowing his strokes, his eyes locked on hers. "Talk tae me, lioness."

"I—" She met his eyes, a tumult of emotion in her own, before she closed them once more. "I need you to give me my release. Please."

He suspected there was something more she wasn't telling him, something she was holding back, but when she began to undulate against him, his desire seized every one of his senses until he could no longer think, and he let out a groan as their mutual release claimed them.

"What were ye going tae tell me, lass?" he asked, when the world righted itself around him again, and he'd caught his breath.

"Just what I told you," she said, giving him a smile that didn't reach her eyes. "That I needed my release. And you gave it to me."

When she nipped at his ear, whispering that she wanted him to take her again, his desire for her quelled his unease that she might be hiding something, and his body once again stirred to life as he claimed her mouth with his.

CHAPTER 22

*E*velyn had come dangerously close to telling Latharn she loved him last night. She was glad she'd held her tongue; she had to remind herself that her confession of love would have only complicated things. Instead, she'd communicated her feelings for him with her body. Latharn had made love to her once more before leaving her chamber, as she shuddered and quaked in the aftermath of their lovemaking.

As she made her way to the great hall the next morning, her hand floated to her mouth; her lips still felt swollen from Latharn's kisses. She flushed; it would be difficult to remain stone-faced around him today.

"Eibhlin."

Evelyn turned, stiffening with surprise as Ros approached her. Latharn's betrothed was lovely in a fine crimson gown, her dark hair tied up in decorative plaits, adorned with white ribbons. She looked every inch the fourteenth-century Scottish noble-woman Latharn needed to marry: nothing like her, a twenty-first century American time traveler who didn't belong here. Her giddy thoughts of last night vanished as that familiar swell of jealousy arose in her chest. She believed that Latharn bore no true affection toward the other woman, but her love for him made it difficult to see reason.

"My lady," Evelyn forced herself to say, giving her a respectful nod.

But Ros waved away the formality, giving her a warm smile.

"Please, call me Ros. Will ye walk with me?"

Evelyn bit her lip, debating offering some excuse. But she finally relented; it would look suspicious if she displayed any ill will toward Latharn's betrothed. Ros beamed, and together they made their way out to the courtyard.

"I wanted ye tae ken, there is nothing between Latharn and I," Ros said, when they were yards away from the castle, speaking in a low tone. "There is another man I love, and I ken Latharn loves ye."

Evelyn looked at her in surprise. She hadn't allowed herself to hope that Latharn returned her feelings. She knew he desired her, but he'd never expressed deeper feelings than that.

"He wants me, aye," Evelyn said. "But—"

"I ken love when I see it," Ros interrupted. "We're both fortunate my father doesnae recognize such emotions. Last night, at the feast . . . it was as if there was a thread no one else could see, linking the two of ye across the great hall. I could see how much ye love him."

Evelyn started to protest, to deny her feelings— but it was no use. Ros was clearly perceptive, and Evelyn knew that any protest she uttered would ring false.

Ros was giving her a look of genuine warmth and kindness. After the way Ros's mother, Lady Reuda Creagach, had treated her, she'd expected the same dismissive snobbery from Ros. She now felt silly for her jealousy. She wondered if things had turned out differently and she'd lived in this time, would her path have crossed with Ros? And if so, would they have become friends? She suspected they would.

"I hope that ye get tae be with yer beloved," Evelyn said, offering her a smile.

But Ros's smile faded, sadness lurking in her eyes.

"Ye donnae get much choice in who ye marry when ye're the daughter of a chieftain," Ros said.

Evelyn's heart softened with sympathy as she thought of the limited choices highborn women of this time had. But then she recalled Latharn's words to her from weeks before. *Ye make what ye can of yer place in life.*

"Well, perhaps ye can make what ye can of yer place in life," she said, echoing his words. "And find some way tae be with him. I ken Latharn will help if he can."

"I hope so," Ros murmured. "And I hope ye can be with Latharn as well."

"Highborn men must also marry lasses of the appropriate class," Evelyn returned, with a sad smile of her own. "My father may have been a noble, but he's long dead and considered a traitor by Clan MacUisdean. I'm a mere—"

She stopped walking as a sudden thought occurred to her. Ros was the daughter of the chieftain and seemed to take a liking to her. Evelyn bit her lip as she studied Ros, wondering how she should broach the subject. Ros arched a curious brow.

"What is it, Eibhlin?"

"May I ask for yer help with something?" Evelyn asked.

MOMENTS LATER, Evelyn sat opposite several noble wives in a private chamber, who studied her with barely concealed distaste.

Evelyn turned to Ros, who gave her an encouraging nod. She'd asked Ros to introduce her to some noble wives who were staying in the castle after last night's feast. She'd failed with Ros's mother, Reuda, but she wanted to sway these women to Latharn's side.

"I thank ye for seeing me," Evelyn said, facing the women. "I wanted tae talk tae ye—we both wanted tae talk tae ye—about yer husbands swearing fealty tae Latharn."

She'd known it would look suspicious if she and not Latharn's betrothed pleaded on his behalf; Ros had agreed to join her.

"I may have only kent my betrothed for a short time, but I believe he is a man of honor. Far more honorable than Padraig. We want ye tae speak tae yer husbands if they still doubt him—and assure them of this," Ros added.

The women's faces softened as Ros spoke, and Evelyn had to tamp down a rush of envy. *It's just for show,* she told herself. *She's not really going to marry Latharn.*

But wouldn't Ros be the perfect match for him? She was compassionate and seemed to hold the respect of the other nobles. If Latharn wasn't going through with his betrothal to Ros because of his desire for her, wasn't she doing him more harm than good? Should she put her love for him aside, and encourage him to wed Ros before returning to her own time?

Pain tore through her at the thought, and she reminded herself that Ros was in love with another man and didn't want to wed Latharn. And now that Evelyn knew how love felt, she couldn't imagine being forced to wed another man when her heart belonged to another.

"We respect ye and yer father," one of the wives was saying to Ros. "But my husband and the other nobles at least ken Padraig. My husband never kent Latharn's father. All we ken of Latharn is that he was a servant."

"Aye," Evelyn interjected. "But I can tell ye what Latharn has done. He's taken the time tae meet with the common folk tae assure them he'd be the best laird for them. He came tae rescue me and several others working for him as spies when he could have been captured and killed. He risked coming tae these lands kenning he could be killed. If he thought that Padraig was a good leader he would have stayed away, even kenning that meant giving up his rightful lands, his rightful titles. Do any of ye ken a leader who would make such a sacrifice?"

The women looked quietly surprised—and impressed. She realized then that many didn't know to what extent Latharn had gone to reclaim his titles.

"Eibhlin speaks the truth," Ros said. "Please consider what she's said when ye speak with yer husbands if they still doubt him."

"Ye did well," Ros said, after the women filed out of the chamber. "The way ye spoke for him . . . 'tis clear how much ye love him."

Panic coursed through her veins. "Do ye think the other wives noticed that I—"

"No," Ros assured her. "They ken who yer father was; they think ye're speaking out of loyalty tae him."

"I am," Evelyn said. "And . . ."

"Latharn," Ros said gently. "I ken. Ye're fighting for the men ye love."

Ros's WORDS echoed in her mind during that night's feast as she watched Latharn and Ros seated at the head table, battling with her envy. It did feel like she was fighting for Latharn: fighting her love for him. Would it get easier once she was back in her own time, centuries away from him? *No*, she realized, her stomach lurching. *It will only be more painful when we're forever separated.*

The guests soon got up to dance, and she focused on drinking her ale, not wanting to watch Latharn and Ros dance. She felt a hand on her arm, and looked up to find Crisdean gazing down at her with a gentle smile.

"A dance, my lady?"

She obliged, noticing with suspicion that his eyes were twinkling. His smile widened, and she realized that he was maneuvering her toward Latharn.

They effortlessly switched partners so that Crisdean was dancing with Ros, and she found herself in Latharn's arms. She met his eyes, sparks of electricity colliding within her belly at the look of raw hunger in their dark depths.

"I sent my brother tae fetch ye," he confessed. "I missed ye today."

"I missed you too," she returned, her heart soaring at his words.

"Tonight," he said, his breath fanning against her ear. "I'll come tae yer chamber."

He released her, and there was an odd look of regret in his eyes before he turned to dance with Ros. Evelyn pushed aside her unease at the look, her body humming with anticipation and desire.

When the feast was over and the castle fell silent, she paced restlessly in her chamber until her door slid open.

Latharn entered, crossing the room toward her without a word, lifting her in his arms as he branded her mouth with a searing kiss. She returned it with a moan, and he carried her to the bed where they made love with a quiet intensity that caused a thunderous climax to claim them both.

Afterward, as they lay entwined, she reached up to trace his handsome features with her fingers. She ached to tell him the depths of her feelings for him; she was tired of hiding them. Evelyn opened her mouth to confess her love, but at the look of regret in his eyes, dread splintered her heart.

"What?" she whispered.

"Ros and I will have tae keep up the appearance of the betrothal for longer than I anticipated," he said with a sigh. "There are still clan nobles who need convincing tae ally with me. While we're staying here, I cannae risk coming tae yer chamber anymore."

Pain clenched her chest, but she gave him a jerky nod.

"Of course. I understand."

"Tis not what I want," he murmured, reaching out to stroke her hair. "But this alliance—"

"You don't have to explain," she said, sitting up and covering her chest, suddenly feeling very vulnerable and exposed. "I said I understand. You should go."

Latharn looked shattered, his handsome features creasing with a frown.

"I want tae spend the night at yer side before I—"

"No, you were right. How do you think the chieftain would react if he knew you were coming to my chamber? You shouldn't spend the night here."

A tumult of conflicting emotions played across his face. He reached out, tugging her close as he claimed her mouth in a brief kiss. She was the one who ended it, looking away from him.

"What I said before still holds, Evelyn. While ye're in this time, ye're mine. As I'm yers."

She nodded, though she only felt a hollow ache inside, watching as he dressed and slipped out of her chamber.

It didn't seem as if he belonged to her. He belonged to his duties, to the clan he would one day rule. Most importantly, he belonged to this time: a time that wasn't her own. And despite her love for him, she needed to remember that.

CHAPTER 23

*R*egret coursed through Latharn over the way he'd left Evelyn the night before. She'd looked so shattered when he told her he could no longer visit her chamber while they were at the castle. It was far from what he wanted, but he couldn't risk losing the alliance; there were now the lives of his men to consider. Still, he would have given anything to take the look of hurt off her face.

But yer time together is temporary, he reminded himself. Soon, the vastness of time would separate them. Perhaps it was best to prepare for that now.

He had to force the image of Evelyn's shattered face from his mind as he entered the great hall to meet with his men, Modan, and Modan's nobles.

"My laird," Gormal said, standing to greet him with a smile as he approached. Gormal had been more jovial ever since Latharn had agreed to wed Ros. "We were just discussing the number of men ye now have on your side. With the men ye've gathered, Artair Dalaigh's men, and the men from Chief Creagach's clan, we have enough men tae attack within the fortnight. We still have some of the chieftain's nobles tae convince, but on the whole, we now have enough men tae take on Padraig."

Latharn met his brother's eyes, who seemed to understand the importance of this moment, giving him a solemn nod. This was the moment he'd been waiting for since he'd arrived—the moment he had enough men on his side to take on his cousin.

"'Tis best if we have a surprise attack," Latharn said. "Padraig kens we're going tae attack, but not when. 'Tis will be tae our advantage tae take him by surprise."

He spent more time discussing battle strategy before the men dispersed, leaving Latharn alone with Modan. Modan stood, giving him a nod of respect.

"It brings me joy that my Ros will marry someone as brave as ye," he said. "She's seemed happier as of late—I believe that's because of ye."

"Ros has made me happy as well," Latharn said, not meeting his eyes as he spoke the lie. "I wanted tae thank ye again for allying with me. I ken 'tis of great risk tae ye."

"There are still some of my nobles tae convince," Modan said, his expression darkening. "But I will make them join ye if they want tae remain loyal tae the clan."

Unease prickled the base of his spine; Latharn

didn't want anyone to join his side by force. But he couldn't tell Modan how to handle his own men.

"I believe victory is at hand for ye," Modan continued. "I want ye tae wed my Ros shortly after the battle is won."

It took great effort to meet Modan's eyes and nod, though panic spiraled through him. If Modan didn't accept his offer of another noble marrying his other daughter, what if he'd have no choice but to wed Ros? Images of Evelyn raced through his mind: her beautiful body in his arms, her smile, her golden eyes lighting up with delight at the sight of him. It felt like a betrayal to even consider wedding another woman, even though Evelyn would soon return to her own time.

As he left the great hall, the sound of Evelyn's musical laughter stopped him in his tracks. He turned, noticing that she was standing close—too close—to Tulach at the far end of the corridor.

When had they become so friendly? Or had they always been friendly? His gut churned—was there something more going on between them? And if so, how had he not noticed it before?

When Tulach pulled Evelyn into his arms for an embrace, Latharn stalked toward them, a fierce scowl on his face. They turned to face him as he approached; Tulach gave him a hasty nod. He ignored him, his focus on Eibhlin.

"I need tae talk tae ye," he bit out.

Evelyn blinked at him in startled surprise. He noticed with irritation—and a spark of lust—that he could see the tantalizing view of her bosom in the green gown she wore. Had Tulach enjoyed the same view?

With a growl he grabbed her wrist, leading her away from the startled Tulach and into a small antechamber, closing the door behind them as he glowered down at her.

"What?" she asked, panic flittering across those lovely features of hers. "Latharn, what is it?"

"Ye and Tulach," he snapped. "Is there something between the two of ye?"

Her surprise vanished, and that familiar defiance flared in her eyes. If he weren't so angry, he would have felt a swelling of pride. His lioness.

"How dare you ask me such a thing?" she snapped. "You are the one who is betrothed, who told me ye were going tae stay away from—"

"I'm not truly betrothed, and ye ken it," he barked. "Now answer the—"

"Have you already forgotten that you said we need to keep our distance here? If people thought Tulach and I were lovers that would lift any suspicion off us."

He couldn't stop the growl that escaped from his throat at her casual mention of her and Tulach being lovers. He leaned in close, only a hairbreadth away from her sensual lips, lips he wanted nothing more than to kiss.

"If Tulach lays a finger on yer lovely body, I'll—"

"Don't threaten Tulach! He's been a loyal spy

for you, and he's my friend. How dare you—especially after what you said last—"

"I also said that ye're mine while ye're here, as I am yers," he snapped, though a sliver of guilt encircled his gut. She was right about Tulach's loyalty, but he wouldn't tolerate him with Evelyn. He couldn't tolerate any man with Evelyn.

"Latharn, you're not being reasonable," she said, her tone softening. A pained look entered her eyes. "I know that your betrothal to Ros is just for show, and I like her, but now you see how it feels for me. Imagine if you had to watch me and Tulach pretend to be betrothed—and ponder us actually being married, me in his bed. And imagine if I told you we had to stay away from each other while doing so."

The jealousy that tore through him was powerful, and he clenched his fists at his sides.

"I ken I'm not being reasonable," he said. "And what I told ye last night—'tis not what I want. As soon as we're out of this castle, ye'll be in my bed every night—until ye return tae yer time." He had to force these last words out, anguish twisting his gut at the thought of her departure.

He couldn't stop himself from leaning in to kiss her, and Evelyn's mouth seemed to melt beneath his. Need and desire for his lioness flooded his senses, and he held her close as he plundered her mouth with his, as if he could claim her with his kiss. When he released her, they were both breathless.

"Do ye understand me?" he rasped. "We belong tae each other."

"Understood," she whispered, her golden eyes aflame with desire.

～

HE TRIED NOT to stare at Evelyn during that night's feast, but he couldn't help himself. After their passionate confrontation, he'd had his duties to tend to and hadn't seen her for the rest of the day until now. He was like a moth drawn to a flame when it came to gazing at his Evelyn. And that is what he thought of her as—his Evelyn. Even if he didn't truly have a claim on her, the sight of her with Tulach had brought his possessiveness roaring to life.

He rarely noticed what lassies wore, but with Evelyn he noticed every detail. She'd brought several gowns with her; tonight, she'd changed into a gown as blue as the summer's sky, the swell of her breasts prominent beneath its bodice.

"Why donnae ye just bed the lass right here for everyone tae see?" his brother murmured in a low voice.

He scowled at Crisdean, who sat at his side, but he quickly turned his gaze to Ros, giving her a polite nod. She only gave him an amused smile; she fully knew of his preoccupation with Evelyn.

"Ye cannae keep yer eyes off Ros's sister," Latharn returned.

Crisdean flushed. It hadn't escaped his notice that he'd kept casting surreptitious glances toward Sofie, Ros's bonnie younger sister, who sat at the opposite end of the hall with her ladies.

"She's a bonnie lass," he grumbled.

"As is Eibhlin," Latharn said, his eyes again straying to her with a scowl as she threw her lovely head back and laughed at something Tulach said.

"I'm not the one who's supposed tae wed the chieftain's daughter," his brother grumbled, and Latharn had no retort; he was right. For the time being, he needed to appear utterly devoted to Ros.

Latharn looked around the hall; the atmosphere was relaxed and jovial, his men easily mingling with Modan's men. He slid his glance back toward Evelyn, who was looking at him, but she averted her gaze when he met her eyes.

He wanted to dance with her, to feel her in his arms, but he forced himself to remain at Ros's side, and dutifully walked her out of the hall after the feast was over to the visible approval of her father.

It took great effort to not go to Evelyn's chamber that night, forcing down his arousal at the memory of her in that blue gown, her flame-red hair flowing down her shoulders to the curve of her luscious breasts.

When he finally drifted off, he heard startled shouts and cries outside the castle.

He shot up in his bed, his heart hammering with panic. He raced to the window to see at least two dozen men approaching the castle on horseback.

Latharn whirled as his door flew open. Crisdean and Horas stood in the doorway, their faces white with panic.

"Padraig kens ye're here," Crisdean said. "We've been betrayed."

CHAPTER 24

*L*atharn raced away from Creagach Castle on horseback, Evelyn seated behind him, her arms wrapped securely around his waist. Crisdean, Horas and Gormal flanked them, and his other men trailed behind, their horse's hooves pounding furiously on the ground.

Half of his men had remained behind to fight alongside Modan's guards. He'd wanted to stay and fight alongside them, but he'd had no choice but to flee. Padraig wasn't with the men he'd sent to attack the castle, and Latharn needed to face his cousin directly in the larger battle to come.

Before he'd fled the castle, he'd raced to Evelyn's chamber, ignoring Horas's protests that his men would get her out. He wouldn't leave until Evelyn was at his side.

He'd fled the castle with Evelyn's hand in his. For all his frustration and fury, he was glad that she was at his side; he never would have left her behind. He could feel the rapid thump of her heart-beat against his back as they rode; her fear was palpable.

Latharn tightened his grip on the reins, his fury rising. He never should have let his guard down. He knew that some of Modan's nobles were hesitant about joining him; he hadn't suspected that they would betray his whereabouts to Padraig. Horas had told him that Modan was furious and surprised at the betrayal; he was fighting alongside his guards against Padraig. Latharn was uncertain of the state of their alliance. Would the nobles who'd sworn their loyalty to him now go back on their word?

They rode until it was nearly dawn, and they were at the far northern edge of Clan Creagach's lands. The cottage where they were to hide out wasn't the fine manor they'd stayed at before, but the home of one of his men, a smith by the name of Sgaire who kindly offered it to him. Sgaire would stay in the nearby village with a relative; his home was large enough to house Latharn, Horas, Gormal, Crisdean and Evelyn. His other men would stay in the village or set up camp on the surrounding grounds.

As Evelyn and the others entered Sgaire's cottage to settle in, Latharn remained outside, watching the rising sun cast its light over the horizon. He needed a moment alone to take in the air and calm the simmering fury that still scorched his veins.

He was weary of running, weary of trying to convince men of his worth. He'd been so close to striking, to facing Padraig on the battlefield and taking back what was his by right. But now, there was yet another setback.

Latharn closed his eyes, expelling a shuddering breath. What if he was destined to fail? Perhaps he'd never reclaim his father's lands. Perhaps he should have stayed away.

"I know what you're thinking."

He turned. Evelyn approached him from behind, a plaid cloak wrapped around her body to ward off the chill of dawn. His body hummed with awareness the way it always did at the very sight of her, but he turned away to face the horizon.

"Ye should go inside and sleep, Evelyn."

"So should you," she returned, stopping at his side. Although they'd been riding all night, she smelled of lavender and rosewater; her scent calmed his senses. "You're doubting yourself, I can see it in your eyes. You had to know this wouldn't be easy. But you're so close. Don't give up."

"I willnae," he muttered, not wanting to admit to her his self-defeating thoughts from moments earlier. Even if he wanted to, he couldn't turn back now. Though some of Modan's men had betrayed him, he still had scores of men who'd sworn their allegiance to him. He wouldn't let them down. And he couldn't let a snake like Padraig lead Clan MacUisdean.

"I need tae stop running," he muttered.

"Padraig will only keep hunting me down. I'm going tae send for Artair and his men. 'Tis time tae fight."

Evelyn nodded her agreement. "And . . . I know you don't want to hear this, but you need to consider what I and the others have suggested about Neacal. He could be an ally and change the tide for you."

He stiffened but forced himself to consider her words. Even Modan had mentioned that Neacal had honor. When Ailbeart was spying for him, he'd told him that Neacal didn't seem interested in leadership—he'd even seemed opposed to his brother. It was a great risk to reach out to Neacal, but he needed every advantage he could to defeat Padraig. And wasn't leadership about making risky decisions?

"We'll have tae be careful," he said finally. "I'll talk tae the others and get a message tae Neacal."

Evelyn smiled. She reached for him, winding her arms around his neck and pressing her lips to his in a fervent kiss that he hungrily returned. When she released him, her golden eyes were alight with emotion.

"You have no idea how frightened I was when I heard Padraig's men attacking the castle," she whispered. "I feared he'd capture you." She lifted his hand to her lips, closing her eyes briefly as she murmured, "I feared I'd never get to tell you how much I love you, Latharn. So I'm telling you now. I love you, Latharn MacUisdean. With every part of my being. I didn't realize it until your betrothal to Ros . . . but I think I've loved you from the start. Do you want to know something? Years ago, when my mother told me about the babe that Seoras and his wife lost, I felt a little spark in my belly. It was like some part of me *knew* that I was meant to love you. That I already loved you. And my love for you will never waver . . . even when I'm back in my time."

And before he could respond, his body shaking with emotion at her confession, she turned and disappeared into the cottage.

WHEN LATHARN WENT TO SLEEP, it was a brief and restless one. It wasn't the battle to come that consumed his thoughts but Evelyn's quiet confession of love. *It was like some part of me knew that I was meant to love you. That I already loved you. And my love for you will never waver.*

Joy flooded his body at the memory of her words, but uncertainty chased away his joy. He didn't know the status of his betrothal to Ros now that Modan's nobles had betrayed him. Even if their alliance was over, he'd still have to wed a well-connected noblewoman to secure his claim. Evelyn's father had been well respected, but he was long dead, and many of the nobles would only ever see her as a servant.

But none of this mattered. Evelyn wasn't from this time; she had added that caveat to her confession of love. *Even when I'm back in my time.* She needed to return to her own time where she'd be safe. What if he hadn't gotten to her chamber in time the night before? What would Padraig have done to her if he'd captured her this time? The thought hardened his resolve; he knew what he would tell Evelyn when he next saw her.

Evelyn wasn't in the cottage when he awoke not long after falling into a fitful sleep; Horas informed him she was training with Tulach and the other men. He frowned at this, but he shouldn't have been surprised. His lioness was fierce, but he wouldn't allow her to fight in the upcoming battle.

"I've sent word tae Artair—and tae Neacal," Gormal said. Gormal had looked hesitant when he'd told him to reach out to Neacal, but he hadn't put up much of an argument. He seemed to understand that they needed any advantage they could gain, even if it was risky.

Gormal informed him that many of Modan's men had joined them; Modan had held off the attack and fortified his castle to ward off any further attacks from Padraig, with some of his men staying back to help him defend it.

"But he's kept tae his word," Gormal said, "and stuck to the alliance despite the betrayal of his men."

Latharn gave Gormal a nod of agreement before leaving to speak to his men who'd set up camp on the grounds nearby.

"I'll no longer flee from Padraig. The time has

come tae fight. More men are joining us—we go tae battle in two days' time."

His men let out shouts of fierce agreement, and determination melded with pride swelled within him; he needed to succeed on behalf of his men.

When he sought out Evelyn, he found her in a large forest clearing with Tulach and several of his men—*she* was the one teaching them archery. He watched with both pride and amusement; he didn't know how she'd convinced these burly Highlanders to let a lass train them, but they listened intently as she demonstrated. Longing coursed through his body as he watched his lioness, and his chest tightened at the thought of what he was about to do, but he made himself step forward.

His men stopped and turned to face him, giving him nods of respect. Evelyn whirled, surprised, her face flaming as she saw him. He knew she was thinking of her confession of love to him that morning; embarrassment infused her expression.

"I'd like tae speak with Ev—with Eibhlin alone for a moment," he told his men.

Once he and Evelyn were alone, he approached her, cupping the sides of her lovely face.

"Evelyn." He swallowed, forcing himself to say the next words. "I want ye tae leave. Tae return tae yer time."

She looked at him in disbelief, her body going stiff with anger as she took a step back.

"I already told you—"

"I ken what ye've told me. But ye've already been imprisoned once, and I've been betrayed. If something goes wrong the third time, I donnae ken what I would do if ye came tae harm."

Evelyn shook her head, her golden eyes glistening with angry tears.

"I tell you I love you, and your response is to tell me to—"

"I'm telling ye tae go because I love ye!" he shouted.

Evelyn froze, her eyes widening. He stared at her, breath heaving, as he continued, "I've loved ye since before yer confession. Perhaps I've loved ye since ye first came tae me, spitting fire out of yer eyes and demanding I let ye help me. Or perhaps since the first moment my lips touched yers—or when I claimed ye with my body. I love Eibhlin Aingealag O'Brolchan *and* Evelyn Angelica O'Brolchan. Ye're the first thing I think of in the morning. The last thing I think of at night. I love ye with every part of my soul, Evelyn. And that's why I want ye tae go. I love ye tae much tae see ye suffer. If ye ever came tae harm again, it would break me, and none of this would matter. So ye have tae go, my lioness. My love."

CHAPTER 25

*E*velyn's heart swelled at his words. Ever since her confession she'd chided herself for telling him how she felt, convinced he didn't feel the same way. But the look he was giving her now was filled with nothing but genuine affection. Nothing but love.

"Latharn—"

"I love ye," he repeated. "And that's why ye must—"

Evelyn silenced him with a kiss. He stiffened for a moment before returning it, enfolding her in his arms as their mouths melded together, their hearts beating in tandem.

When she pulled back, he kept her in the circle of his arms.

"You've tried to send me away before," she gently reminded him. "And I'm going to say to you the same thing I said then—I'm staying until the battle is won, and you've earned your titles back. Only then—only then will I leave and return to my time," she said, anguish tearing through her at the thought.

Though Latharn loved her, his duties hadn't changed. Once he became laird and chief, he would have to wed a suitable bride, not the daughter of a long-dead clan noble who now worked as a servant.

A storm of conflicted emotions passed over his face, but he gave her a jerky nod.

"I kent ye would refuse, but I had tae try," he whispered. "I love ye so, my Evelyn."

Joy soared in her chest; she'd never tire of hearing him say the words. He reached out to wind his hand in her hair, pressing her close for yet another kiss that left her breathless. She clung to him, desperate to remember every single detail she could about this moment.

When he released her, they returned to the cottage together for the midday meal. But as they drew near, Evelyn stiffened; a small group of men approached the cottage on horseback.

"Stay here," Latharn ordered, leaving her behind as he hurried forward to join Horas, Crisdean and two of his other men as they stood protectively before the cottage.

Dread tightened her chest as she moved to the doorway of the cottage, praying that these weren't Padraig's men.

The men stopped several yards away, and one of them dismounted. He was a slight man who didn't look like a clan noble but a peasant, with a worn wool cloak, white tunic and tattered, dirty breeches.

"Are ye Latharn MacUisdean?" he asked Latharn.

"Aye," Latharn returned.

"Who are ye?" Horas demanded, moving to stand in front of Latharn. "How did ye ken where tae find us?"

"Common folk have spread word that Seoras MacUisdean's son has returned and will remove Padraig as laird," the man replied, turning to Latharn. "Padraig has raised the rents; many cannae pay. Now that people ken ye're back, they're no longer willing tae cower before the current laird. We wish tae join ye in yer fight against him—if ye'll have us."

Relief swirled through Evelyn as Latharn stepped forward with a smile, moving past Horas to clamp the man on his shoulder.

"I'll be honored tae have ye."

The men who arrived were only the first of several groups to arrive, all with the same tale of word spreading that Seoras MacUisdean's son was about to go to battle with their current laird. Evelyn watched with pride as Latharn greeted and welcomed each man who joined him before they set up camp with his other men. He'd often meet her eyes, and she would give him an encouraging smile. People were now seeing what she already knew—that Latharn would make a far better leader than Padraig.

Evelyn spent the rest of the day training some of Latharn's men in archery. Tulach and Horas had spread word of her prowess, and while many men refused to take lessons from a lass, others were willing to set their pride aside to improve. She realized that this was something she could do when she returned to her own time, she truly enjoyed it—though an avalanche of pain swept over her every time she thought about leaving Latharn.

Through all this, the matter of Neacal lingered in the back of her mind; he hadn't responded to the message Latharn had sent to him through a messenger, and she feared that she'd been wrong about Neacal.

If Latharn shared the same concern, he didn't express it with her; he already had much on his mind with the upcoming battle. That night Latharn ushered her into his room, but they didn't make love, speaking little as they just held each other close.

As she drifted off to sleep, she tried not to think of the upcoming battle, of the possibility of losing Latharn, but she couldn't help but think of her mother and her life of grief. Now that she'd fallen in love with a man from the past, she could understand her mother's eternal sadness. Evelyn knew that she too would never recover if Latharn fell in battle—or after she'd left him behind.

WHEN SHE AWOKE, it was to the sound of horse hooves approaching the cottage. Latharn was already gone, and she hastily dressed before slipping out of his room.

Latharn stood outside the cottage, along with Gormal, Horas and Crisdean, a broad smile on his face as a handsome man with wavy chestnut hair dismounted from his horse, along with a lovely blond woman. They had roughly fifty men on horseback behind them; Evelyn realized this must be Artair and his wife, Diana.

As Artair strode toward Latharn, Diana studied Evelyn for such a long, disconcerting moment that Evelyn wondered if she knew her.

"Laird Latharn MacUisdean," Artair greeted Latharn, clamping him on the shoulder. "I was happy tae receive yer letter."

"I thank ye for coming," Latharn said, returning Artair's smile.

"I meant what I told ye—I'll always assist ye in any way I can."

Latharn made introductions, and as he and Artair headed inside the cottage, and Artair's men dispersed to set up camp, Diana approached her.

"Evelyn. It's nice to meet you," Diana said with a warm smile.

Evelyn stiffened with surprise; the woman had an English accent—a modern, twenty-first-century English accent. Her instincts had been correct.

This woman had to be a time traveler. As if sensing her surprise, Diana gave her a wry smile.

"I think we have much to discuss."

~

MOMENTS LATER, Evelyn walked along the edge of camp with Diana, reeling from all that she'd just told her. Not only was Diana a fellow time traveler from the twenty-first century, she was a stiuireadh. She told Evelyn how she'd only agreed to help guide Artair back to his time after a distant descendant, Niall, had taken his place. She hadn't expected to fall in love with him and remain in this time, especially when she'd turned her back on magic and time travel for much of her life.

"And you?" Diana asked.

As Evelyn told her her story, Diana listened intently, shaking her head in amazement.

"It's rare for someone born in the past to live in another time period," Diana said. "I sensed you were coming . . . that you would appear in Latharn's life."

"You did? How?"

"Even I don't understand how it works. It was just a feeling I had, every time I was around Latharn." She stopped walking, studying Evelyn with disconcerting focus. "You love him, don't you?"

"Yes," Evelyn replied without hesitation. There was no need to dance around her love for him, especially after they'd discussed time travel, witch-craft and magic. "But it doesn't matter."

"Love is the only thing that matters," Diana gently returned. "One thing I learned growing up around stiuireadh . . . love is the strongest force that can permeate through time. It's even stronger than magic."

"But Latharn needs to marry someone suit-able," Evelyn said, avoiding her intense gaze. "I don't want to hinder him."

"I understand," Diana said. "But you can never hinder someone who loves you as much as Latharn does. I can sense his love for you with just a glance."

Evelyn's heart warmed at her words. She and Diana spent the rest of their walk discussing the things they missed and didn't miss about the twenty-first century, and the things they enjoyed during this time.

"The quiet," Diana said. "There's nothing like living in this time to realize how bloody *loud* the future is."

Evelyn laughed, nodding her agreement. That had struck her during the first and second time she'd traveled through time as well; she much preferred the quiet of the past over the hubbub of the future.

"But most of all . . . Artair. He's the reason I stayed here. I think I always knew deep down that I was meant for him," Diana said.

Evelyn's gut twisted; she felt the same way

about Latharn. But the time in which he lived had a different set of rules.

Her heart was heavy as they made their way back to the cottage. Before they reached it, Diana turned to face her, squeezing her arm.

"Titles and land aren't the only things worth fighting for," Diana murmured cryptically, before turning to head inside.

CHAPTER 26

*A*fter Latharn and Artair spent time with their men discussing the next day's battle strategy, they went for a ride to the far end of camp where they could speak in private.

Latharn had many questions for Artair about Diana, and Artair confirmed what he'd suspected. Diana was not only a time traveler but a stiuireadh, one of the time-traveling witches Evelyn had described.

"Traveling through time," Latharn murmured, shaking his head in amazement. "How is it possible?"

"I donnae ken. Neither does my wife," Artair said with a rueful smile. "But I'm glad 'tis possible. Otherwise, I would have never met my Diana. She is my life's love. Without her, my life would have been empty."

Latharn's chest tightened; he felt the same about his Evelyn. When she disappeared through the fabric of time, he knew he'd never love a lass again. How could he after Evelyn, his lioness? She was a lass like no other.

"I'm proud of what ye've achieved," Artair was saying, glancing back toward his camp of men. "'Tis difficult tae get men tae follow ye, especially when they've never kent ye. They must ken what I do— that ye're a good man. A worthy leader."

Pride and relief swelled within Latharn; he didn't realize how much he wanted his former laird's approval until now.

"I hope I can be the leader they deserve," he said. "I've no choice but tae win this battle. If we suffer a loss, I'll not forgive myself. I'll gladly go tae my death."

His heart stung as he thought of Evelyn and leaving her behind. Knowing his lioness, she might even refuse to leave this time even after his death; she'd do something brave and foolhardy like trying to get revenge. "Can I ask something of ye, Artair?"

"Aye," Artair said, studying him closely. "About yer Evelyn?"

"Aye," Latharn said, enjoying Artair's referral to Evelyn as "his." "If I fall in battle—"

"Donnae say such—"

"If ye were tae fall, ye'd want tae ken yer Diana was taken care of, aye? Just . . . look after her. Please. Make certain she's safe. I'll ask my brother tae do the same."

"I will, but donnae think of defeat before going

in tae battle," Artair said, after a long pause. "Think only of victory."

When they made their way back to camp, he longed to share a meal alone with Evelyn, but he had an obligation to his men; they were risking their lives for him.

He ate his supper with them instead, trying to spend as much time as possible with each cluster of men, listening to their stories and why they'd joined him. He heard personal tales of low food stores after a difficult winter, higher rents that paid for the elaborate feasts Padraig liked to enjoy, illnesses and deaths of beloved family members because of the low food yield. Anger coursed through him at the tales. He promised himself he'd do right by each and every man, woman and child of Clan MacUisdean.

At the end of the meal, he stood and faced his men.

"Remember when ye fight tomorrow, 'tis not just for me, but for yer rights, yer clan. And when we have our victory, I will be a fair laird and chieftain; I will never forget that I once toiled like each of ye have. As yer leader, I will always fight for ye."

His men let out a chorus of grateful cries and shouts of agreement. He met Evelyn's eyes in the crowd; she stood at the edge of it next to Diana, giving him a smile tinged with pride.

He approached her as his men dispersed. Diana left them alone to approach Artair, and he pulled Evelyn close.

"I want tae spend the night before battle with ye, my lioness," he whispered, pressing his head against her forehead.

"And I you," she whispered.

He smiled and took her hand, walking with her back to the cottage.

"My laird."

He halted in his tracks, stiffening in surprise as Horas approached, grasping the arm of a hooded man. When they drew near, Horas threw back the man's hood, revealing a dark-haired man with angular features. Next to him, Evelyn let out an audible gasp.

"Neacal," she breathed.

Neacal gave her a brief nod, his gaze sliding to Latharn.

"Hello, cousin," he said calmly.

"I DIDNAE want tae believe that my brother was as cruel—crueler—than our father," Neacal said darkly.

They were now back in the cottage; Latharn sat opposite Neacal while Horas hovered next to him, his hand on the hilt of his sword. Evelyn, Artair, Diana, Gormal and Crisdean all stood behind Latharn; he could feel their eyes trained on Neacal.

"But I've seen what he's become," Neacal continued, expelling a sigh. He turned to glance at Evelyn before his focus returned to Latharn. "I didnae ken my brother had imprisoned Eibhlin; I was away and would have stopped him. He imprisons not just suspected spies but anyone who challenges him. Raising the rents for the sake of his greed. Assaulting the female servants and encouraging his men tae do the same. Inciting other clans tae battle. With him as laird and chief, Clan MacUisdean will only suffer bloodshed. 'Tis why I fought him for the lairdship—not because I wanted it, but because I saw what Padraig was becoming. Many of the clan nobles donnae respect him—they fear him. From what I've heard of ye, Latharn, ye would be a better leader. The clan would have peace. Ye are the true leader; I'm ashamed of what my father did. I willnae fight my brother on the battlefield, but I will try tae get him tae see reason one last time—tae cede his claim tae ye tae save his life, though I ken he will refuse."

A torn look flickered across his face, and though Latharn tried to keep his heart hardened—this was the son of the man who killed his father—empathy coursed through him. Given his love for his own brothers, he could understand Neacal's turmoil.

"What can ye tell us that will help?" Gormal asked.

"Padraig kens ye're coming, but ye already ken that. He's making the common folk fight, and he's putting them on the front lines—he believes their lives donnae have much worth," he said, his mouth twisting with disgust. "Ye should focus on the men at the rear of his lines—that is where his strongest fighters are." Neacal turned to Latharn. "I hope ye have victory tomorrow, and if ye do, I hope ye'll consider sparing my brother."

"Would he have spared me?" Latharn asked, arching a skeptical brow.

"No," Neacal replied honestly. "But I still ask ye tae consider giving him the *chance* tae surrender. If he doesnae . . . " Neacal swallowed, his eyes filling with pain. "Then I understand that ye'll do what ye must."

Neacal got to his feet. Horas looked at Latharn, his hand tightening on the hilt of his sword, but Latharn gestured for him to stand back.

"Ye're going back?" Evelyn asked, stepping forward.

"I must try tae get my brother tae see reason," Neacal replied.

"What if he kills ye?" she asked, and jealousy prickled at Latharn's chest at the concern in her voice; though she was right. From what he'd heard of Padraig, it wouldn't surprise him if he imprisoned his own brother and sentenced him to death.

"I donnae believe he will. But if he does," Neacal continued, expelling a breath. "Then it shall be done. I should have stopped my brother before."

He started toward the door, but not before turning to give Latharn one last look.

"I'll pray for yer victory tomorrow, cousin. If ye succeed, I'll help convince the others that ye are the rightful leader."

"I thank ye," Latharn said, giving his cousin a nod.

"Do ye trust him?" Artair asked, after Neacal left the cottage.

"Aye," Latharn said. He'd seen nothing but sincerity in Neacal's eyes; he could now see the honor in Neacal that the others had spoken of. He'd thought it impossible that his murderous uncle could have fathered a son who didn't share his cruelty, but now he saw that he was wrong.

When the others dispersed, he took Evelyn's hand, and they entered his room.

"That took great courage, listening to him," Evelyn said when they were alone. "I'm glad you did."

"Ye were right about him," he said. "I should have listened tae ye sooner."

He moved close to her, no longer wanting to discuss Neacal or tomorrow's battle. If he did fall tomorrow, he wanted to savor this last night with his lioness.

"I love ye, Evelyn," he breathed. Her eyes filled with joy and desire as he reached out to undo the bun she'd tied her hair up in, allowing it to spill over his fingers like silken threads.

He pressed his lips to hers as he lifted her into his arms. She wrapped her legs around his waist as he lowered her to the bed, slowly undressing her and drinking in the sight of her nude body.

"I love yer fierceness," he whispered, disrobing before he captured a rosy nipple in his mouth and suckled. "Yer strength. Yer beauty. Yer bravery. Yer kindness. Even yer stubbornness, my lioness."

He punctuated each word with a kiss on a different part of her body: her breasts, her abdomen, her throat.

"Latharn," she whispered, her eyes glistening. "I love you so."

His heart soared at the words; would he ever tire of hearing it? *Never*, he thought. *I'll never tire of hearing it.*

"Say it again," he rasped, entering her in one smooth thrust.

She threw her head back in a moan but obliged, whispering that she loved him as he began to thrust, grasping her buttocks to hold her as close to him as possible. Her words became a litany as they lost themselves in each other, until they reached their mutual climax.

He shuddered, burying his face in her neck, wanting to breathe in the very essence of her, his love—the woman he would always love, even after she vanished through time.

A LIGHT RAIN fell over the glen as Latharn led his men south, his sword clutched in his hand.

It was just past dawn the next morning; he'd learned from his scouts that Padraig's men were approaching from the south. He'd taken Neacal's advice and ordered his men to focus on Padraig's strongest men at the rear of his lines, while Horas, Crisdean and a group of his most loyal men would flank Latharn as he made his way toward Padraig to fight him one-on-one.

Latharn's heart thundered in his chest as he moved. Around him, there was only the sound of footfalls on wet grass, heavy breathing and the patter of raindrops against the ground. A group of archers trailed them on the east, ready to cover them when the battle began.

Latharn allowed himself to enjoy a brief memory of Evelyn: her soft skin against his, her words of love, before he tucked away the memory in the most private place in his heart.

A sudden roar rose in the distance—it was the sound of horse hooves and men's cries as they charged into battle. His heart picked up its pace as he turned, shouting at his men to charge.

They obliged as Padraig's men materialized in the distance, racing toward them with battle cries. Latharn took in the front lines. Neacal had spoken the truth; the men who charged toward them looked lowborn with their old, tattered clothing and simple weapons.

Latharn's men followed his orders and focused their attention on moving toward the rear of the attacking men, where Padraig's strongest warriors fought. Latharn expertly fought off the men who approached him, flanked by Horas and Crisdean.

His heart leapt into his throat as he heard more shouts, and he whirled. More of Padraig's men descended upon them from the west. His men weren't prepared, and he heard startled grunts and cries as they were overtaken.

His archers sprang into action, and a flurry of arrows showered down onto Padraig's charging men.

"Forward!" Latharn cried amid the din. "Charge forward!"

But it was chaos, with his men now acting in defense rather than offense, struggling to fight off Padraig's encroaching men. He could see Artair through the din of bodies urging his men forward.

He whirled, searching through the mass of fighting bodies until he spotted Padraig at the rear of his men, flanked by half a dozen guards. Fury raced through him at the sight of the snake, and he let out a snarl and charged forward, only to be stopped by a large, burly man whose sword clashed with his. As they fought, Crisdean ran to his side.

"Go!" his brother shouted. "I'll hold him off!"

Latharn obliged, charging forward, fighting off attacking men as he did. Once he drew closer to Padraig, his cousin met his eyes and stiffened.

"Kill him!" Padraig ordered his guards.

Did the coward not want to take him on himself? Latharn growled as Padraig's guards charged; Horas and Latharn's other men darted forward to help him fight them off. He knocked out two with the hilt of his sword and stabbed another straight through before darting toward his cousin.

As soon as he reached Padraig, their swords

clashed in midair. Despite his cowardice, Padraig was as good a fighter as Latharn, and their swords met blow for blow, until Padraig reached out with a snarl, knocking him backward with his foot. Latharn lost his footing, slipping on the ground which had become muddy with rain, his back hitting the ground with a painful thud as Padraig lunged forward, lifting his sword to land the killing blow.

But an arrow sailed through the air, nearly piercing Padraig in the neck. Padraig dodged, avoiding it, which gave Latharn enough time to shoot to his feet.

Moving as fast as his body would allow, he reached for his sword, kicking at Padraig's knees and sending him sprawling to the ground. Padraig reached for his sword, but Latharn caught it, clutching both swords as he glowered down at his cousin, pressing his foot to his throat.

"I give ye this one chance, cousin," he shouted, over the din of battle around them. "Cede yer claim. Order yer men tae lay down their weapons. And I'll let ye live."

"Never!" Padraig roared, his eyes flashing with hatred.

Latharn gritted his teeth, lifting his sword to deal the death blow, but Padraig moved fast, twisting away. He shoved Latharn to the ground with his leg, and Latharn was once again on his back, the impact so sharp that the world spun around him.

Padraig grabbed one of the fallen swords, straddling Latharn as he lowered the blade toward his chest—

But Latharn wrapped his hand around the blade, ignoring the pain in his hand as it bled, using all his strength to keep it from piercing his heart.

"Ye should be dead already!" Padraig roared, his face turning red with effort as he worked to press the blade down. "Ye shouldnae have survived! My father left the clan tae me!"

At the mention of his uncle, the man who had killed both his father and the father of the woman he loved, Latharn's rage swelled, giving him a surge of strength. Using his free hand, he reached down to grab his dagger, still in its sheath at his side, jutting it upward and into Padraig's throat.

Padraig's eyes filled with fury, then surprise, then pain, as his body jerked, and blood spurted from his wound. And then he went still, his body slumping forward onto Latharn, his eyes wide—and unseeing.

CHAPTER 27

*E*velyn stood on the edge of camp, watching as the sea of men returned from the battlefield. She waited with bated breath, her heart a battering ram against her chest, praying that Latharn had survived.

Diana stood at her side, her face pale; Evelyn knew she was just as terrified for Artair. She'd wanted to help turn the tide of battle for Latharn's men with her magic, but Artair had insisted that she stay behind.

Swallowing hard, Evelyn reached for Diana's hand, and they stood in tense silence, two time travelers on the edge of a fourteenth-century battlefield, waiting for the men they loved to return.

Please, Evelyn prayed, watching as the men drew closer. *Please let him be alive. Please.*

She noticed that the men's faces were weary—but triumphant—as they returned. But she couldn't find Latharn in the crowd, and her panic swelled . . . until she spotted his familiar form.

He and Artair walked side by side, their clothes soaked with rain and blood. Artair was limping while Latharn was clutching his injured hand, but they were both alive.

A strangled cry erupted from Evelyn's lips. She didn't care who was watching; she darted forward, throwing her arms around Latharn and pressing her lips to his. Latharn returned her kiss, holding her close.

Latharn would later tell her that after he killed Padraig on the battlefield, many of his men, especially the peasants who'd only fought for him out of fear, had defected, turning the tide of battle in his favor.

But for now, Evelyn only wanted to focus on the fact that Latharn had survived the battle and was here in her arms.

"I love you," she whispered, tightening her hold on the man she loved, never wanting to let him go.

IN THE BATTLE'S AFTERMATH, Latharn took up residency in MacUisdean Castle. The nobles of the clan swore fealty to him, with Neacal's support. Padraig's top nobles were imprisoned when they refused to swear their loyalty; but most seemed happy to see Padraig gone, confessing that they'd only served Steaphan and then Padraig out of fear.

Latharn had kept to his word and convinced Modan to allow his other daughter Sofie to wed Crisdean, who'd become quite taken with her during their stay at Modan's castle. Modan had also allowed Ros to wed the man she loved, the son of his castle's groomer. Modan seemed pleased with this arrangement; it was an attractive prospect to have one of his daughters wed to the brother of the new laird. But that meant that the clan nobles were now vying to have Latharn wed their daughters, sisters or nieces.

Artair and Diana left the next day, but not before Diana asked to take a walk with Evelyn around the courtyard.

"When do ye plan to return to Tairseach?" she asked.

"Tomorrow," Evelyn said, an ache piercing her heart at the thought. "Latharn will officially be made chief and laird at a celebratory gathering tomorrow, and then I'll have Horas escort me south."

Diana studied her closely.

"Is that what you want?"

"It's the only choice I have. You know what this time is like; the rules are different. Latharn's just become laird, he needs to marry someone acceptable."

"I'm pregnant."

Evelyn stilled. While she was happy for Diana, she didn't know why she'd chosen to share such news at this moment.

"I'm happy for you," Evelyn said, giving her a smile. "Congratulations."

"It's why Artair didn't want me to help on the battlefield. The reason I tell you this now is because I was like you once—uncertain of my place with Artair. I knew I wanted to stay with him, more than anything, but fear held me back. Had I left and returned to my time . . . " Diana's face tightened with anguish. "I can't imagine my life without him."

"Artair was already a laird by the time you met him," Evelyn reminded her. "My situation with Latharn is different."

"We're both women who traveled back in time and fell in love with sexy Highlanders," Diana returned, giving her a wry smile. "I don't think our situation is too different. Just . . . think about what I've said, all right? If returning to the future is what you truly want, then make sure it's with an open heart."

Diana's words echoed in her mind as she returned to her chamber. She knew she wouldn't return to her own time with an open heart; she'd be leaving behind the man she loved. But she'd already heard the other nobles suggest highborn brides to Latharn, proving her point that he needed to marry someone suitable, not a time traveler from the twenty-first century.

She entered the castle, stiffening as she noticed Gormal approaching her. She expelled a breath; he was likely going to ask her to leave the castle now that Latharn was laird, and her services were no longer needed.

"I'm leaving after the gathering tomorrow," she said stiffly, once he reached her. "There's no need tae tell me tae leave."

Gormal looked at her with surprise and shook his head.

"I wasnae going tae ask ye tae leave. I wanted tae apologize," he said gruffly. "For how I've treated ye. I kent yer father, and I respected him; I'd have angered him had he kent how I treated his daughter."

Evelyn just looked at him in silent astonishment, not believing that he was actually apologizing. He gave her a rueful look.

"Ye're not the only one I've offered my apologizes tae. I also apologized tae Latharn for my imperiousness. I was so determined tae see him become laird, and I kent what a good leader he'd be. When ye came around, I feared he'd lose focus. But ye only seemed tae help him focus."

"I thank ye," she said, offering him a smile. "And I accept yer words of apology."

Gormal relaxed, returning her smile. It was odd to see the older man, who'd spent the last few weeks glowering at her, give her a genuine smile.

"I also came tae see ye because the laird wanted me tae summon ye. There's someone who wishes tae see ye in the great hall."

Evelyn trailed him into the great hall, freezing in surprise at the sight of Aimil standing before

Latharn, her head bowed low. Latharn gestured for her to come forward and she obliged, facing Aimil.

"I wanted tae beg yer pardon in the part I played in yer imprisonment," Aimil said, her face filled with shame, still not looking at her. "Padraig had imprisoned the man I love, my betrothed, for not being able tae pay his rent. He told me he'd show him mercy if I spied on the other servants when rumor spread that Latharn MacUisdean had returned. He—he asked me tae follow any servant who was new and took long absences from the castle. I remembered that ye'd asked about Laird MacUisdean being alive, so I followed ye during one of yer visits tae see him; 'tis how I kent ye were a spy. I—I didnae want tae tell Padraig, but if I hadnae told him something, he'd have killed my betrothed." Aimil closed her eyes, tears spilling. "If ye want tae imprison me, tae exile me . . . I understand."

Latharn's mouth tightened, but he looked at Evelyn.

"I'll let ye decide," he muttered.

Evelyn studied Aimil, her heart warming with sympathy. She knew what it meant to do anything for the man you loved.

"I understand, Aimil. Ye're forgiven," she said gently.

Evelyn looked at Latharn, who gave her a grudging nod.

"Ye'll return tae yer post, but if ye ever seek tae

betray me . . ." Latharn told Aimil, his voice trailing off with warning.

"I willnae," Aimil said. She looked up at Evelyn, shaking as she wiped her eyes. "I thank ye, Laird MacUisdean. Thank ye, Eibhlin."

As Aimil left, Latharn turned to her and started to speak, but he was interrupted by another noble.

"Laird MacUisdean, I was hoping we could continue our discussion about ye wedding my niece, Ceit. She's a fine lass who—"

Evelyn turned and hurried out of the hall, not wanting to hear anything more about his potential bride, anguish swirling in the depths of her stomach.

You will leave before he marries someone else, she reassured herself. She'd done what she came here to do, and Latharn was in his rightful place. She could nurse her broken heart when she returned to her own time.

EVELYN DIDN'T SEE Latharn for the rest of the day. A new laird was a busy man, with a stream of visitors and nobles either swearing fealty or asking him for favors. She remained in her guest chamber, telling herself she needed to rest before embarking on the trip to Tairseach—and back through time. But she knew she was only fooling herself. She wanted to avoid hearing about Latharn's new bride.

She remained in her chamber even during

that night's feast; Aoife brought her meal to her room, where she ate alone, trying not to think about who Latharn had chosen for his bride, and trying not to wonder why he hadn't sent for her— or visited her chamber—before she fell into a restless sleep.

By the time she awoke the next morning, she decided that she couldn't stay for tonight's celebratory gathering. The gathering would be a perfect place for Latharn to announce whom he'd chosen to wed, and her heart couldn't take even hearing the name of his future bride.

She left her chamber after washing and changing into a gown comfortable enough for travel, her heart heavy. She had to find Horas to escort her south to Tairseach. She couldn't face Latharn to say goodbye; it would break her heart to face him.

Evelyn stepped out into the corridor, freezing as she saw Crisdean approaching her chamber.

"Where are ye going, lass?"

"I'm leaving," she said, forcing a smile. "I—I should return home. I've stayed longer than I intended."

"My brother wants tae see ye in the great hall," Crisdean said with a frown.

"Send him my apologies, but I should—"

"Please, Evelyn," he said, and she started, looking at him in surprise at the use of her real name. "My brother may have told me some things about ye," he added, with a knowing look. "But after this, ye have my word I'll escort ye tae Tairseach if ye donnae want tae stay."

She swallowed hard. Had Latharn told Crisdean she was a time traveler? And what did Latharn want with her in the great hall?

After a brief moment of hesitation she nodded, trailing Crisdean down to the great hall.

When she entered, an ache spiraled through her at the sight of Latharn standing at the head table, surrounded by the nobles in all his finery: a dark tunic and a belted plaid kilt, no longer the humble servant but the laird and chieftain he was always meant to be.

His eyes met hers as she sat down at one of the long tables in the back of the hall next to Crisdean.

"As ye all ken, I must marry someone with strong ties to one of our allied clans—or one of yer kin, now that I am laird and chief," Latharn said.

Evelyn's heart lurched with pain, and tears stung her eyes. Is this why he'd wanted her to come to the great hall? Was he going to make her listen to him announce his bride?

"I'm here tae announce who I've chosen tae wed."

Evelyn's eyes swam with tears. She lowered her head, her stomach lurching. She got to her feet, needing to get away. Crisdean reached out to stop her.

"Evelyn—"

"I can't listen to this," she whispered, her heart too shattered to keep up her accent. She moved past him, tears spilling from her eyes. "I—have to go."

"My betrothed's father once served this clan under my father, and he died for his loyalty. His daughter is fierce, proud, and strong. So fierce I've called her by the name of those creatures who dwell in faraway lands. Lioness."

Evelyn was halfway to the door, but froze at Latharn's words.

"She is the strongest lass I've ever kent. Many of ye have seen for yerselves how fierce she is as an archer. She's risked her life for me—for this clan—by spying for me in this castle, toiling as a servant, undergoing torture when she was captured. But she kept fighting for me. Her father was a man ye all respected, a clan noble, yet she worked as a servant without pride. I want tae be a great leader for ye, but I can only be that leader if I have Eibhlin Aingealag O'Brolchan at my side—or Evelyn Angelica O'Brolchan, as her English mother called her, the name she prefers. Evelyn, the woman I love. And for those reasons, I choose her as my bride. My lady. If she'll have me."

Evelyn slowly turned, her mouth dry. All eyes in the hall were trained on her.

Latharn stepped out from behind the table, approaching her, his eyes filled with raw emotion.

"If she'll have me," Latharn continued, as he approached her, "this brave lass will bear the MacUisdean name. My name. I choose her; there is no one worthier than her. 'Tis I who isnae worthy of her. But I hope she'll accept my proposal." He knelt before Evelyn, taking both her hands in his. He spoke in a low tone now, for her ears only. "Will ye stay with me in this time and be my wife, Evelyn? All that I am, all that I have . . . 'tis yers. Including my heart."

Evelyn met his eyes, her heart thundering in her chest, a joy she'd never known before sweeping over her. In his eyes, she saw love. In his eyes, she saw her future.

"Yes," she whispered. "I love you so, Latharn MacUisdean."

Latharn beamed, standing to lift her into his arms as the nobles shouted words of approval and congratulations, punctuated by shouts of "Lady MacUisdean!."

But Evelyn was only aware of Latharn; the man she loved. Her present, her future. Her always.

"I love ye," he whispered, his eyes locked with hers. "My Evelyn. Lady MacUisdean. Ye are my destiny."

EPILOGUE

One Month Later

Kensa watched from the rear of the great hall as Evelyn and Latharn were wed, their eyes locked on each other with love as they spoke their vows. She smiled as the priest announced they were now husband and wife; Latharn pulled his new bride into his arms for a passionate kiss as the guests cheered.

Her gaze trailed from Evelyn and Latharn to two other couples that time, fate and magic had brought together; her niece Diana and Diana's husband Artair, along with Niall and Caitria, who all sat at the same table, beaming as they watched Evelyn and Latharn seal their vows with a kiss.

Artair turned to Diana, his hand lowering to his

wife's belly, which was just beginning to swell with the early stages of her pregnancy. Niall and Caitria locked eyes, and Caitria reached out to link her hand with Niall, who raised it to his lips, pressing a tender kiss on her palm.

Kensa had spent the last fortnight checking in on the couples that had been pulled together across time. Eadan and Fiona, who were now tucked away in Macleay Castle, happy parents to a newborn daughter. Kara and Eadan's cousin Ronan, who often shared dinners with Eadan and Fiona, and took long walks along the path outside Ronan's manor. Ciaran and Isabelle, Fiona's close friend whom Fiona visited as often as she could, who was now in the latest stage of pregnancy with their first child. She'd watched Ciaran and Isabelle walk hand in hand through the courtyard of Aitharne Castle, Ciaran's hand often drifting protectively to his pregnant wife's belly, a smile of love spreading across his handsome features.

Watching the love that had pulled these couples together across centuries brought Kensa great joy. She felt her niece's eyes on her across the hall, and she gestured for Kensa to join them. It was Diana who'd had Evelyn extend an invitation to her and Latharn's wedding, though Kensa had yet to formally meet her.

Kensa's gaze flicked back to Latharn and Evelyn, who now greeted their guests hand in hand as they were congratulated. From her place in the back of the hall, she could hear that Evelyn's modern accent was starting to come through—ever so slightly. Diana had told Kensa that Evelyn planned to gradually slip back to her native accent over time, using the excuse of the lingering influence of her English mother. But given how the nobles of the clan had taken to Evelyn after she'd help fight for Latharn's titles, as well as their new laird's utter love and devotion to his bride, she suspected that no one would mind.

Evelyn had found her own way to this time, but Kensa had kept careful watch over her during this trip to the past, and the one she'd taken previously to make certain that nothing went awry, prepared to intervene if necessary. But once Evelyn crossed paths with Latharn, she knew it was only a matter of time before love bound the two of them together.

Kensa turned back to face her niece, merely giving her a subtle shake of her head. It was time for her to leave this time and return to the present. She would return from time to time to visit Diana, but she had served her purpose in this time for now.

Kensa took one last look at her couples before turning to slip from the hall without notice, a smile on her face, content that the strings of time, magic and fate had pulled her time travelers to when— and to whom—they belonged.

THE END

~

JOIN STELLA KNIGHT'S *newsletter to be notified of upcoming releases.*

AFTERWORD

The origin of the idea for this series began with a simple image: a woman standing in a museum in modern day Scotland, struck by the familiarity of a painting that was created in the fourteenth century. I wondered—what if the painting caused her déjà vu because *she* was the one who painted it? What if she was a time traveler whose soul mate lived hundreds of years in the past? From there, the story pooled out of me, along with Kara and Ronan's, then Ciaran and Isabelle's, all the way to Evelyn and Latharn's story. I find medieval Scotland utterly fascinating with such a rich, vivid history; it was the perfect time period to send my time travelers back to.

I tried to be historically accurate where possible, but given that this is a historical *fantasy* series featuring time travel, magic and witches . . . I did take some license. The biggest one is the language; Gaelic was the language spoken in the Scottish

Highlands at this time, but given that my modern-day travelers didn't speak Gaelic, I used the distinctive Scottish brogue as a substitute. There was also, sadly, no kilts—at least not the ones we think of today. There was the precursor to the modern day kilt which was an outer garment called a "belted plaid" or a "great kilt" which is why I used the term "belted plaid" whenever I could.

I read many books and sources to delve into the time period, some of the most helpful sources include *Life in the Middle Ages* by Richard Winston, and *The Time Traveler's Guide to Medieval England* by Ian Mortimer, among many, many others.

The clans in the series are all fictional, though I did take some inspiration from the famous age-long feud between the MacDougal and Campbell clans. Tairseach is fictional, but I think it would be fun if a place like that existed . . .

I had help bringing this series to life, and I'd like to take a moment to thank those who did so. I'd like to thank my amazingly talented cover designer, Kim Killion, for her lovely covers featuring the dashing Highlanders of the Highlander Fate series. I'd like to thank my wonderful editor and proof-readers including Paula, my primary editor / proof-reader who is patient, thorough, and efficient. I'd also like to thank the narrator of the audio books, Liisa Ivary, for bringing my characters so vividly to life.

On a personal note, I'd like to thank Mr. Knight

for being such a supporter, cheerleader, and my very own swoon-worthy hero that makes creating dashing Highland heroes a cinch.

But most of all? I'd like to thank each and every reader who stumbled across my books and took a chance on a new-to-them author and dived head-first into my world. Thank you for all your kind messages telling me how much you love the series, the world, and most importantly the characters. I can't tell you how much each message means to me —and how grateful I am to each of you for reading my books. Without you, I would be out of a job— and there would be no Highlander Fate series. So thank you, from the bottom of this grateful author's heart.

I hope that you'll stay in touch. You can join my newsletter, visit my website, or follow me on Facebook or Bookbub to be notified of upcoming releases—and to generally stay in touch. And feel free to drop me a line anytime, I love hearing from readers.

With love and gratitude,

Stella Knight

ABOUT THE AUTHOR

Stella Knight writes time travel romance and historical romance novels. She enjoys transporting readers to different times and places with vivid, nuanced heroes and heroines.

She resides in sunny southern California with her own swoon-worthy hero and her collection of too many books and board games. She's been writing for as long as she can remember, and when not writing, she can be found traveling to new locales, diving into a new book, or watching her favorite film or documentary. She loves romance, history, mystery, and adventure, all of which you'll find in her books.

Stay in touch! Visit Stella Knight's website to join her newsletter.

Stay in touch!
stellaknightbooks.com
stella@stellaknightbooks.com

Made in the USA
Coppell, TX
18 September 2020